# William Shakespeare's Dracula

## IAN DOESCHER

Based on the novel by Bram Stoker

To Tricia and to Sean, my sister and
my brother from another mister/mother.

# DRAMATIS PERSONAE

Mina Murray, *Chorus, later Mina Harker*

Count Dracula, *a vampire*
Jonathan Harker, *lawyer and Mina's fiancé*
Lucy Westenra, *Mina's friend*
Arthur Holmwood, *Lucy's fiancé, later Lord Godalming*
Quincey Morris, *friend and suitor to Lucy*
John Seward, *a doctor and suitor to Lucy*
Abraham Van Helsing, *a professor*
R.M. Renfield, *Dracula's devotee*
Sister Agatha, *nun and caretaker*
Peter Hawkins, *colleague to Jonathan Harker*
Three women, *minions to Dracula*
Captain, boatswain, and crew, *of the ship* Demeter
J.M. Caffyn, *a surgeon*
S.F. Billington, *a solicitor*

Hotel hostess, drivers, asylum attendants, Szgany servants, and various citizens.

**Scene:** Europe, especially London and Transylvania

# Prologue.

*Enter MINA MURRAY as Chorus.*

Mina  Lust—for the fragile taste of human life,
Undying, merciless, unquenchable—
Gone rampant through the arteries of time,
On Europe plying havoc ruthlessly.
Such was the fate of him whom ye shall meet,  5
Insatiate and near unconquerable.
Lust—for the lavishness of human life,
Expressive, hopeful, irrepressible,
Earth made a heaven through camaraderie,
Long-suff'ring, sorely tried, yet tightly knit  10
Amidst uncounted sacrifices to
Necessity—such shall ye witness here.
Give ear unto a group of valiant folk,
E'en those I call mine own, my friends most dear:
Love powerfully overcoming hate.  15
Lust—for the slings and shocks of human life,
Adventure, trepidation, misery—
O'erflows throughout our yearning theaters.
Lo, ye shall see a tale to sate your thirst,
Demanding sights beyond the written word.  20
Mere articles of news should not suffice,
A letter never could contain the fear,
No diary would hold the horror grim
Now proffer'd for your eager, waiting eyes
In this, the three hours' traffic of our stage.  25
Engorgèd shall ye be ere ye depart,
Lips wet with drink, yet longing still for more—
Such is the reason ye have hither come.
Ere ye may rest your souls *in saecula*,
Needs pass through dreaded Castle Dracula!  30

*[Exit.*

# ACT I

# SCENE 1.

### *The road to Castle Dracula.*

*Enter JONATHAN HARKER, writing a letter.*

Jonathan         Ah, when shall we two meet again, my love,
My Mina, second heart unto mine own.
For work calls me from thy side, thitherward
To meet our noble client Dracula.
The coach wherein I speed away from thee     5
Doth make its progress speedily enow—
This Buda-Pesth doth seem a wondrous place,
And mine impression as we journey on
Is that we leave the west and meet the east.
Ere I departed London, 'twas my aim     10
To learn more of this land of Transylvania;
Through knowledge of the country, I may be
Prepar'd for bus'ness with its citizens.
No map, though, gave the slightest hint or trace
Of where this Castle Dracula is found,     15
Though Bistritz, mention'd by the Count, is shown.
The journey hath not been a boon to rest:
The bed was plenty comfortable, and I
Would sleep were it not that I have bad dreams.
Strange dreams, odd dreams, such troubling dreams are
                                mine,  20
That I could think myself a man accurs'd.
There is a dog that howls all night beyond
The window, though, which may well take the blame,
And too much pepper in my paprikash
Did stir my thirst for water all the night.     25
Now come we to the Golden Krone Hotel,
To where Count Dracula directed me.
My love, thou art with me though not nearby,
And I remain thy doting Jonathan.

*He puts the letter away. Enter HOSTESS.*

| | | |
|---|---|---|
| Hostess | Herr Englishman? 'Tis you we should expect? | 30 |

Jonathan    Yea—Harker. Jonathan. The same am I.

Hostess    A message hath proceeded your arrival,
Which you may read, sir, as it pleaseth you.

*[She hands him a note.*

Jonathan    *[reads:]* "*Willkommen*, friend, to the Carpathians.
Most anxiously am I expecting thee.    35
Sleep well tonight. Tomorrow thou shalt ride
To Bukovina, then the Borgo Pass.
There shall my carriage bring thee to my side.
I trust thy journey was a happy one,
And my proud land shall please thy sanguine soul.    40
I am thy friend forever—Dracula."
Pray, hostess, dost thou know this Dracula?
Canst tell me ought of him or of his castle?

Hostess    It is a subject—how say you?—*verboten*.
Herr, must you go? Do you, sir, know the day?    45

Jonathan    'Tis May the fourth—be with thee any else?

Hostess    Sith 'tis the eve of great Saint George's Day,
Tonight the clock shall strike its midnight toll.
Then, as the poet long ago hath writ:
    Grim darkness falleth 'cross the land,    50
    The midnight hour is close at hand,
    When creatures crawl in search of blood
    To terrorize the neighborhood.

> And whosoever shall be found
> Without a soul pure and profound 55
> Shall stand and face the hounds of hell
> And rot inside a corse's shell.

Jonathan  Peace, peace, dear hostess, peace! Thou talk'st of
nothing.
My duty takes me thither in the morn.

Hostess  If you would make but some two days' delay, 60
'Twould be twice better for your tender soul.

Jonathan  Imperatives cannot brook narratives—
I go despite thy tales and needless fear.

*[She unclasps the crucifix on her neck and puts it around his.*

Hostess  Take, then, this token for protection, sir.
Do it, I bid you, for your mother's sake. 65

Jonathan  *[aside:]* The custom of my English church regards
Such things as near enow idolatrous,
Yet 'tis ungracious to deny her plea,
Her state of mind so worried o'er my health.
*[To hostess:]* I'll wear it even as thou sayest, madam. 70

Hostess  Well may it serve you on your eastward ride.
Now, follow—we may warm ourselves inside.

*[Exeunt.*

## SCENE 2.

*The Borgo Pass and Castle Dracula.*


*Enter DRIVER.*


| | | |
|---|---|---|
| Driver | Another body have I render'd to | |
| | The Borgo Pass and that strange place beyond. | |
| | Yea, speak of bodies rather than of souls: | |
| | 'Tis not for me to ponder sacred things, | |
| | 'Tis not for me to question his demands, | 5 |
| | 'Tis not for me to count those who are lost, | |
| | 'Tis not for me to ask why none return. | |
| | I drive the coach, deliver persons here— | |
| | An occupation solemn and covert— | |
| | And am not paid to question what I do. | 10 |
| | Throughout the region, people fear this place, | |
| | And superstition spilleth freely from | |
| | Whoever speaks of Castle Dracula. | |
| | None, though, do know the path from here to there— | |
| | Like Charon guarding o'er the river Styx, | 15 |
| | One guide alone takes bodies further on. | |


*Enter JONATHAN HARKER, emerging from the coach.*


Jonathan        Is this the place?


| | | |
|---|---|---|
| Driver | —Yea, but we come too soon— | |
| | Some hour entire ere we're expected here. | |
| | Perchance this is a sign from fate itself, | |
| | Which chooses safety for your spirit, sir. | 20 |
| | Belike to Bukovina we'll return, | |
| | And try the Borgo Pass another day. | |


*Enter DRACULA, dressed as a coachman, riding in a large, dark carriage.*

Dracula      Tonight thy cargo comest early, friend.

Driver       The English Herr requested utmost haste.

Dracula      Yet thou wouldst take him back to Bukovina?      25
             I see thy mind; thou canst not me deceive.
             I know too much, my horses are too swift.

Driver       *[aside:]* Yea, they say "*Denn die Todten reiten schnell*"—
             Which is to say the dead do travel fast.
             *[To Jonathan:]* I leave you, sir, unto this good man's care. 30

Jonathan     *[aside:]* Thus am I traded like so many goods,
             A strange exchange as ever I did see.

             *[Jonathan gets into Dracula's coach. Exit driver, riding away.*

Dracula      The air doth bear a dreadful chill tonight.
             My master bade me make thee comfortable—
             There is a flask of slivovitz within,            35
             Which, with the hardy blankets thou shalt find,
             Will keep thee warm as we approach the castle.

             *[The coach proceeds through the woods.*

Jonathan     *[aside:]* Despite the call of reason, my heart quakes
             To see the woods and fog, so dark and drear.
             A dog doth wail beyond the racing coach—          40
             Another answers it, now more and more.
             The hills beyond respond with howls of wolves,
             Far worse than those few dogs who cried before,
             A sound to pierce the bravest person's calm.
             Now, through the line of trees—which form a sort   45
             Of tunnel through the thick and frightful wood—
             Wolves run astride the carriage next to us!

|                  | Teeth bony white, their lolling tongues shine red, |     |
|                  | Long sin'wy limbs and ashen, shaggy hair           |     |
|                  | The moonlight, shining on us from above,           | 50  |
|                  | Doth seem to spur the wolves, like whips to backs. |     |
|                  | The horses whinny, tremble, snort, and scream,     |     |
|                  | The coachman urging them with stern rebukes.       |     |
|                  | Ne'er felt I so afeard in all my days.             |     |
| Dracula          | Be calm at once, and get ye gone, ye fiends!       | 55  |
|                  | I send not for you yet—await my call.              |     |
| Jonathan         | What words are these? Ne'er heard I such commands. |     |
|                  | Yet stranger still: the wolves fall back and fade, |     |
|                  | Like ships that meet the mist and dissipate.       |     |
|                  | What power hath the coachman over them,            | 60  |
|                  | That wolves retreat when he doth bid them so?      |     |
| Dracula          | Sir, we arrive.                                    |     |
| Jonathan         | —The castle?                                       |     |
| Dracula          | —Straight ahead.                                   |     |
|                  | Thus I depart, my obligation fill'd.               |     |

*[The coach stops and Dracula-as-coachman exits.*

| Jonathan         | Shall ev'rything, like vapor, disappear?           |     |
|                  | The driver, stealing from the Borgo Pass,          | 65  |
|                  | The wolves, receding from the speeding coach,      |     |
|                  | The coachman, gone without a further word.         |     |
|                  | I stand alone before this castle vast,             |     |
|                  | Whose tall, black windows shed no ray of light,    |     |
|                  | Whose battlements are broken, ruinèd—              | 70  |
|                  | A jaggèd line against the moonlit sky.             |     |
|                  | Of knocker or door-bell I see no sign              |     |

And shouting would not penetrate these walls,
So how am I to make my way within?
What sort of place is this to which I've come?                    75
What sort of people shall surround me here?
What venture grim am I embarking on?
Soft, Jonathan—there is a light within,
A clattering of chains, a clank of bolts,
The rusty swinging of th'imposing door—                    80
The signs of someone come to welcome me.


*Enter DRACULA at the door.*


Dracula        Good welcome, sir, unto my simple house.
               Pray, enter freely of thine own accord.


*[Jonathan crosses the threshold and Dracula moves forward, shaking his hand.*


Jonathan       *[aside:]* How firm the grasp of this most agèd hand,
               As cold as ice and causing me to wince.                    85
               How strange the man who bears the mighty grip,
               Pale visage, clad in black from head to toe.


Dracula        Yea, welcome, friend—come freely and go safely.
               Leave something of the happiness thou bring'st.


Jonathan       Count Dracula?


Dracula               —Yea, Dracula am I.                    90
               All welcome, Mister Harker, to my home.
               The night is chill, and thou must eat and rest.


Jonathan       Pray, trouble not yourself on mine account—

| | |
|---|---|
| Dracula | Nay, sir, thou art my guest. 'Tis very late, |
| | And all my people take their slumber now.      95 |
| | Let me see to thy comfort pers'nally. |

*[Dracula leads Jonathan to a banquet hall.*

| | |
|---|---|
| Jonathan | A supper full, prepar'd for my arrival. |
| | I know now how to thank you. |

| | |
|---|---|
| Dracula |     —Say no more. |
| | Be seated, sir, and sup howe'er thou pleas'st. |
| | Excuse me that I do not join thy meal—      100 |
| | Already have I din'd and drank my full. |

*[They sit together. Jonathan eats.*

| | |
|---|---|
| Jonathan | *[aside:]* His face is strong, his nose an eagle's beak, |
| | Which frame the eyes that seem to search for prey, |
| | His forehead riseth like a lofty dome, |
| | Hair growing scantly round the temples there—      105 |
| | More striking visages I ne'er have seen. |
| | *[To Dracula:]* The meal is more than ample, once more thanks, |
| | Your home is a sensation for the eyes. |

*[A wolf howls in the distance.*

| | |
|---|---|
| Dracula | Behold their cry—the children of the night. |
| | What music they do make! |

| | |
|---|---|
| Jonathan |     —Ah, I confess,      110 |
| | This city-dweller's ears receive a fright |
| | Whene'er their shrieking stabs the calm of night. |

Dracula      The feelings of the hunter are unknown
To those who live within the city's walls.
But, sir, thou must be spent from all thy travels—     115
Thy bedroom is prepar'd, I'll show thee thither.

*[They walk.*

Jonathan      *[aside:]* His cutlery is fashion'd from pure gold,
So beautifully wrought, its worth immense.
The curtains, chairs, and furniture are form'd
From fabric costly and immaculate.     120
Though centuries have pass'd since they were new,
Their value must be near incalculable.
Yet though the home is flawlessly design'd,
There are no looking-glasses anywhere!
    *[Jonathan notices a room of books as they walk the halls.*
*[To Dracula:]* Your library is worthy of a king.     125
Behold these tomes that tell of English life—
Geology, geography, and law,
Political economy and his'try,
Directories of ev'ry London street.
It gladdens me to see these signs of home.     130

Dracula      There's much I'm sure shall int'rest thee, my friend.
These fond companions are good friends to me,
For long have I desir'd to know thy land—
To feel the rush of its humanity,
To share its life, its changes, and its death.     135
Alas, I only know thy tongue through books;
To thee, it must seem I can little speak.

Jonathan      Nay, Count, you speak my English thoroughly!

Dracula      I thank thee, sir, for thy kind flattery.
Were I in London, all would know me for     140

A stranger in a strange land, verily.
Here I am noble, master over all—
So long have I been master that I would
Be master still, and none shall master me.
Thou comest to my home not merely as          145
The agent of my dear friend Peter Hawkins,
To help me with my new estate in London—

Jonathan     Yea, Carfax, from the old name *Quatre Face*,
Because the house hath four sides that align,
Agreeing with the four points of the compass.          150

Dracula     Indeed, but be more than solicitor—
Teach me, please, proper English intonation.
If I make errors as I speak, pray tell.

Jonathan     I am most willing, as you may require.
May I return unto the library?          155

Dracula     Thou mayst go anywhere within the castle,
Except where thou dost find the doors are lock'd.
                              *[They arrive at Jonathan's room.*
Tomorrow, sleep as late as thou desir'st.
I shall be gone until the afternoon,
So slumber well and dream of pleasantries.          160

Jonathan     Your hospitality exceeds my hopes.
I can no other answer make but thanks,
And thanks; and ever thanks.

Dracula                    —Farewell, my friend.

                              *[Exit Dracula.*

Jonathan      The seeming warmth with which I'm welcom'd here
Should give me cause for gladness and relief.      165
Why is my spirit, then, disquieted?
I am all in a sea of wonders here:
I doubt, I fear, I think the strangest things,
Which I dare not confess to mine own soul.
God, if thou watch'st me from thy throne above,      170
Pray keep me, for the sake of those I love.

*[Exit.*

## SCENE 3.

*Castle Dracula.*

*Enter DRACULA.*

Dracula      Within my veins there flows such royal blood
That I, with pride, do roam the earth entire.
My ancestors Hungarian did thwart
Brave races, fighting as the lion fights,
A whirlpool of the European stock:      5
Icelandic blood of Thor and Wodin both,
The mighty men of Afric, Asia too—
Though these be foes most grave, they were repuls'd.
What devil or what witch was e'er so great
As powerful Attila of the Huns,      10
Whose blood doth course within these veins of mine?
The Szekelys, the fam'ly of my line,
Were guardians amid the harshest times:
Of the Four Nations who more gladly did
Receive the bloody sword, or quicker flock      15
Unto the standard of our gallant king?
Who was it but one of my selfsame race
Cross'd o'er the Danube, there to beat the Turk?
'Twas Dracula indeed—again, again,

Throughout the centuries our worth displaying!     20
Our record doth, like mushroom, grow beyond
What Romanoffs and Hapsburgs e'er shall reach—
Their warlike days are done, their blood too precious
In these days of dishonorable peace.
The glories of great races are a tale     25
Already told, complete, and at an end—
Except for mine, whose splendor still shall rise.

*Enter JONATHAN HARKER, shaving, using a looking-glass.*

Good morning, Jonathan, my worthy guest.

Jonathan     *[aside:]* How did the man appear? I saw him not—
The looking-glass was blind to sight of him.     30

Dracula     Alas, it seems I've given thee a fright,
And thou hast cut thyself. Thy poor, dear chin.

Jonathan     'Tis but a scratch, sir, trouble not yourself.
*[Aside:]* Although the man doth stand behind my
                        shoulder,
Again the looking-glass shows naught of him.     35
The room behind me wholly is display'd,
Myself too, but of Dracula no jot.

Dracula     I see the blood that dribbles to thy neck—
*[Dracula reaches for Jonathan's throat, but is stopped by the crucifix*
*                   Jonathan wears.*
Take care how thou dost cut thyself, my friend,
For in this country 'tis more dangerous     40
Than in thy native England, by my troth.

Jonathan     My thanks, sir, for your generous concern.

| | |
|---|---|
| Dracula | Hast thou writ Peter Hawkins recently? |

| | | |
|---|---|---|
| Jonathan | Nay. Since the day I first arrivèd here, | |
| | I've not been giv'n the opportunity. | 45 |

| | |
|---|---|
| Dracula | Write now, young friend, and say, if it doth please, |
| | That thou shalt stay with me a further month. |

| | |
|---|---|
| Jonathan | So long? |

| | | |
|---|---|---|
| Dracula | —Yea, no refusal I'll accept. | |
| | When thine employer sent thee for mine aid, | |
| | 'Twas understood my needs alone would reign. | 50 |

| | |
|---|---|
| Jonathan | As you do say, so shall I humbly write. |

| | |
|---|---|
| Dracula | Pray, let thy discourse be of naught but bus'ness— |
| | 'Twill please thy friends to know that thou art well, |
| | And thou art eager to return to them. |

| | | |
|---|---|---|
| Jonathan | *[aside:]* So must I take great pains with what I write, | 55 |
| | For he shall read the letter ere 'tis sent. | |

| | | |
|---|---|---|
| Dracula | One further thing: let me advise thee, friend, | |
| | Leave not thy rooms to slumber somewhere else | |
| | Within the castle, for 'tis very old | |
| | And doth contain abundant memories | 60 |
| | That may result in most unpleasant dreams | |
| | For those who sleep unwisely. Be thou warn'd! | |

*[Exit Dracula.*

| | | |
|---|---|---|
| Jonathan | Count Dracula hath access granted, such | |
| | That I may wander through the castle's halls, | |
| | Yet ev'ry door is lock'd and bolted shut. | 65 |

My days are spent in poring o'er his books
And wishing for the day I shall depart.
Yet when I peer beyond my chamber's window
I see the horror of my situation:
The castle's built upon a precipice,                    70
A fortress at the rooftop of the sky!
A stone that fell from this most dreadful height
Would fall a mile sans touching anything.
The eye sees only forest, gorges, chasms,
A wilderness uncrossable and vast.                      75
The castle is a veritable prison,
And I am prisoner! O, can it be?

                    *[He looks out the window.*

Yet, even as I speak I see the man—
Not coming through the doorway like he should,
But far below, upon the castle's ramparts.              80
Although his face is hid, his cloak spread out,
I know him by his neck and how he moves.
He crawleth—O, he crawleth!—on the stones,
His toes and fingers grasping at the rock,
And moveth downward with amazing speed                  85
An 'twere a lizard creeping o'er a wall.
What manner of a man is this? Or, worse,
What creature in the semblance of a man?
The dread of this foul place comes over me,
Encompass'd by such terrors all around!                 90


*Enter THREE WOMEN.*


Woman 1       Come, my friends, and we shall greet,
                  He who bringeth fresh-cut meat.


Woman 2       To him, sisters, let us slink—
                  Who shall be the first to drink?

| | | |
|---|---|---|
| Woman 3 | Thou the eldest, be thou first, | 95 |
| | Satisfy thy burning thirst. | |

Jonathan     Is this a dream, or are there women here?
My soul grows faint, my body suddenly
Rack'd by a sleepiness I ne'er have known.
Upon the bed, quick! Lay upon the bed—    100
There shall I rest and cease this reverie.

*[He lies down on the bed.*

Woman 2    See him wither, looking wan,
Shrinking, weak—how like a man!

Woman 3    Eyelids, as the half-moon, close.
Lie back, take a passive pose.    105

Woman 1    We shall fill thine ev'ry wish,
We thy stewards, thou our dish.

Jonathan    How I desire to kiss their lips of red,
Voluptuous and longing for my skin!

*[The women crawl on the bed with him.*

Woman 3    Young and strong the man appears—    110
We shall all have kisses, dears.

Woman 1    Like an animal to prey,
With him shall I have my way.

Woman 2    We shall taste his body's wine.
Friends, the time hath come to dine.    115

Jonathan      Her tongue doth lick her white and pointed teeth,
Her breath a furnace on mine eager neck.
I burn with craving, merciless and rare—
O, ladies, take me anywhere ye will!

*Enter DRACULA.*

Dracula      Ye harpies, get ye swiftly from my guest!      120
*[Dracula grabs the women, pulling them away from Jonathan.*
He is not thine for supping—leave him be!

Woman 3      Master, shall we be displac'd?
Grant your servants but a taste!

Dracula      How dare you touch him, any of you? Shame!
You were forbidden clearly—back, I say!      125
The man belongeth solely unto me.
Beware before you meddle with his fate,
Or consequences shall ye face anon.

Woman 1      Shall we be rebuk'd and shov'd,
By a man who never lov'd?      130

Dracula      Yea, I have lov'd, as ye know from the past.
I promise ye, when I have done with him,
Then may you kiss him even as you will.
Yet ere that time doth come, more work remaineth.

Woman 2      Shall we nothing have tonight?      135
But one taste, sir! But one bite!

Dracula      Take ye this morsel to fulfill your needs,
Yet leave the man until the time is ripe.

*[He throws a sack to the women. Exeunt women, feeding on the contents*
*of the sack. Exit Dracula severally.*

| | |
|---|---|
| Jonathan | Although they thought me sleeping whilst they talk'd, |

Jonathan    Although they thought me sleeping whilst they talk'd,
        Mine ears heard all—their thirst unnatural,   140
        The Count's assurance that I would be theirs,
        The whimper of a child within the sack
        Before the sirens set upon their meal.
        Come sleep, and bear me speedily away!
        O horror, horror past all understanding—   145
        Hope dying whilst the terror is expanding.

*[Exit.*

## SCENE 4.

### *Borgo Pass and Castle Dracula.*

*Enter various CITIZENS.*

Citizen 1    Didst see the man who at the castle stays?
        Methought I saw him yesterday, in town.

Citizen 2    Yea, 'twas him, certainly. I saw the cloak
        In which he is most frequently array'd.

Citizen 3    He carried many letters, I am told,   5
        Which were address'd and bound for merry England.

Citizen 1    Yet when I saw him, he had not the gait
        Of that same man who travel'd through at first.

Citizen 3    Think'st thou the man is alter'd in some way?

Citizen 2    Perhaps the castle works its magic on him?   10

Citizen 1  Of magic or of marvels I know none,
      Yet could, in court of law, swear to these words:
      The man who wears the clothes is not the same
      As he who pass'd, by carriage, through our town.

Citizen 2  A mystery to add to the mystique     15
      Of that foreboding castle on the cliff.

Citizen 3  Come, let us discourse share of pleasant things—
      Of kindness and goodwill, not frightful tales.

*[Exeunt.*

*Enter JONATHAN HARKER.*

Jonathan  God help me; I am surely in the toils.
      Last night, the Count bid me write letters three:  20
      One saying that my work was nearly done,
      And I should start for home in some few days,
      One saying I should leave upon the morn,
      As though departure were anon assum'd,
      One that I had already left the castle    25
      And wrote from Bistritz, safe and homeward bound.
      Fain would I have rebell'd, yet madness 'tis
      To quarrel with the Count whilst in his pow'r,
      Which is o'er me, at present, absolute.
      I would not, by refusal, spur his anger.    30
      He knows I know too much and must not live,
      Else I shall prove most dangerous to him.
      Mine only chance is to prolong my days,
      Find opportunity for an escape.
      He smoothly reassures me that these notes  35
      Will ease the feelings of my fretful friends,
      And will be held until such time as I

Make my departure from this awful place.
I join the pretense, like we two are children
Who mount a trifling play for merriment.                    40
The truth is clear, though, to both me and him,
And when I ask'd what dates he'd have me write
Upon the letters three, he answer'd thus:
June twelfth, June nineteenth, June the twenty-ninth.
Methinks I know the span, now, of my life.                    45


*Enter DRACULA, holding a candle.*


Dracula        My friend, thou hast a busy writer prov'n.
               The letters three thou gav'st to the Szgany—
               My servants, Transylvanian residents
               Who lend me their protection loyally—
               Yet in the midst of those, there is a fourth.          50


Jonathan       Another letter did you find? How strange.
               What are its contents? *[Aside:]* Thus, our play resumes.


Dracula        Thou knowest nothing of it, I presume?
               The letter is unsign'd and horrible,
               A vile thing, outrage unto friendship and             55
               The hospitality that I have shown.
               It is an aberration, some foul deed
               Writ by a fiend; it cannot matter to us.


                              *[He uses the candle to burn the letter.*


Jonathan       A worthy end for such betrayals, sir.


Dracula        Indeed! Thy letters, though, are sacred texts,         60
               And shall pass safely unto England's shores.
               Pray, take thy rest and sleep in perfect peace.

*[Exit Dracula.*

Jonathan My hidden letter is discoverèd,
 Which tells me the Szgany are no allies
 And that small hope I held is swiftly dash'd. 65
 My liberty must take a diff'rent shape;
 I shall find other means for mine escape.

*[Exit.*

## SCENE 5.

*Castle Dracula.*

*Enter DRACULA and a MOTHER on the grounds of the castle.*

Mother Yet will you give me satisfaction none?
 Thou monster, give to me my child most dear!
 Thou tookest him for purposes most bleak—
 Where is he, fiend? What hast thou done with him?

Dracula Be gone, else thou shalt know a worser fate! 5

Mother What fate is worse than when a loving mother
 Is cheated of her offspring heartlessly?

Dracula Thus shalt thou learn.

*[He makes a howling sound and exits.*

*Enter a pack of WOLVES.*

Mother  —O man unnatural,
 Who calleth on the very hounds of hell
 To do his bidding, that he may depart 10
 And let the beasts fall to his handiwork.

See how they salivate with hunger strong,
Hear how they growl, preparing for the hunt,
Smell that foul stench of murderous intent.
This is the chase: O, I am gone forever.                    15

*[Exit, pursued by a wolf.*

*Enter JONATHAN HARKER.*

Jonathan          With weary eyes I witness'd how the Count
                  Called on his forest denizens and brought
                  That poor, unhappy mother to her end.
                  Yet 'tis not all, much more have I discern'd.
                  I have not seen the Count in daylight yet—        20
                  Can it be that he sleeps when others wake,
                  That he may be awake whilst others sleep?
                  Today, midst bright of sun, I action took:
                  I stole throughout the castle, searching in
                  The places I ne'er ventur'd to before.            25
                  I found a ruin'd chapel, old and grim,
                  Which is turn'd graveyard. There were boxes laid—
                  Some fifty boxes brought unto the castle
                  By those whom Dracula doth call his servants.
                  In one of those foul caskets lay the Count!       30
                  Amidst the brown dirt, freshly dug, he lay,
                  Yet whether dead or sleeping I knew not.
                  His eyes were open, stony, staring straight,
                  But did not shine with glassiness of death.
                  His cheek was warm, his lips as red as e'er,      35
                  Yet though I long survey'd, no movement came—
                  No pulse, no breath, no beating of the heart.
                  Now night doth fall again, and 'tis the date
                  Of my last letter. In my clothes array'd,
                  The Count hath taken pains to prove 'twas writ    40
                  By mine own hand, and thus my end draws nigh.

*Enter DRACULA.*

| | |
|---|---|
| Dracula | Tomorrow, friend, we part. Thou shalt return |

Dracula      Tomorrow, friend, we part. Thou shalt return
             Unto thine English home, I to my work,
             Whose end is such that we may never meet.
             Thy letter home is carefully dispatch'd,            45
             And in the morn thy journey shall begin.

Jonathan     If all is ready, why not go tonight?

Dracula      So swift an exit is impossible—
             My coachman and my horses are away.

Jonathan     Fain would I walk, to start the trek anon.           50

Dracula      What of thy baggage?

Jonathan               —I care not for it.
             Send it another time by other means.

Dracula      You English have a saying I hold dear:
             "Welcome the coming, speed the parting guest."
             Not one small hour shalt thou spend in my home     55
             Against thy will, though thou hast made me sad
             To suddenly desire departure. Hark!
             What is that melody that fills the air?

             *[The sound of wolves' howling is heard.*

Jonathan     *[aside:]* The rogue, his subtle messages are clear:
             I may go free, if I would face his hounds          60
             And meet the selfsame end the mother met.
             *[To Dracula:]* I'll wait until the morn, as you suggest.

*[Exit Jonathan.*

*Enter THREE WOMEN.*

| | | |
|---|---|---|
| Woman 2 | We are patient far too long, | |
| | Let us sing a supper song. | |
| | | |
| Woman 3 | This thirst, master, we must sate, | 65 |
| | Wherefore do you make us wait? | |
| | | |
| Woman 1 | We must have the red delight— | |
| | We must have the red tonight! | |
| | | |
| Dracula | Back, back, to your own place! Your time comes not— | |
| | Have patience, for tonight is mine alone. | 70 |
| | This evening I'll have dinner with our guest, | |
| | Tomorrow night may ye enjoy the rest! | |

*[Exeunt.*

*Enter JONATHAN HARKER on balcony.*

| | | |
|---|---|---|
| Jonathan | I rose this morn, astonish'd I should be | |
| | Alive to see the sun another day. | |
| | A wild desire o'ertook me to obtain | 75 |
| | The key unto the castle, damn the risk. | |
| | Unto the dreadful chapel I return'd, | |
| | Where Dracula did sleep, his countenance | |
| | Appearing younger than it had before. | |
| | I seiz'd a shovel, striking at his face— | 80 |
| | Yet as I did, his eyes fell on me with | |
| | The blazing fire of creeping basilisk. | |
| | I heard his workmen coming, and I fled. | |
| | My final glimpse was of his bloated face, | |
| | Bloodstain'd and fix'd with grin of malice pure. | 85 |

Unto his chamber, his own room, I've come.
The sounds of servants moving caskets is
A hammer on the temples of my brain.
Soon shall I be alone with those foul women!
I shall not stay to try my fate with them,          90
But shall attempt to scale the castle wall
Much farther than I hitherto have tried.
Thus may I find escape from this foul place,
And then to home, to Mina, to my love.
The precipice beyond is steep and high,          95
Be swift and brave—God, help me now to fly!

*[Exit.*

# ACT II

## SCENE 1.

### *The Westenra home, London.*

*Enter MINA MURRAY on balcony.*

| | | |
|---|---|---|
| Mina | My dearest Lucy, friend and confidant— | |
| | I long for our upcoming northward trek, | |
| | Where we, in Whitby, shall talk freely and | |
| | Build castles in the air to reign as queens. | |
| | Of late have I been working fervently, | 5 |
| | To keep abreast of Jonathan's own studies— | |
| | I practice shorthand constantly, that I | |
| | May one day be his worthy stenograph. | |
| | Belike I shall turn lady journalist, | |
| | One who doth interview, write full accounts, | 10 |
| | Recalling ev'ry conversation's turn. | |
| | With little practice, I am told, one may | |
| | Remember ev'ry word one heareth spoken. | |
| | Of Jonathan, my love, I have some news: | |
| | A letter from him recently declares | 15 |
| | He is quite well, and shall be home anon— | |
| | One week, perchance, till he shall make return. | |
| | Yet what of thee, sweet Lucy? Rumor swirls | |
| | With tantalizing whispers, speaking of | |
| | A tall and handsome man with curly locks? | 20 |

*[Exit.*

*Enter LUCY WESTENRA and ARTHUR HOLMWOOD,*
*in the drawing room of the Westenra home.*

Lucy     Didst thou enjoy the concert yesternight?

| | | |
|---|---|---:|
| Arthur | The music was delightful, well perform'd, | |
| | And yet methought the company was better— | |
| | A harmony to make composers weep. | |
| | | |
| Lucy | Thou flatterest e'en as the stringèd harp, | 25 |
| | Arpeggios and flourishes thy tricks. | |
| | | |
| Arthur | Nay, I am solid as the double bass, | |
| | Upon whose low notes one could cities build. | |
| | | |
| Lucy | And I a trilling flute above the rest? | |
| | | |
| Arthur | Thou, dear, art wholly violin to me— | 30 |
| | The player of the sweetest melodies, | |
| | The most refin'd and marvelous of strings, | |
| | The leading part in any symphony, | |
| | The instrument that soars above the rest. | |
| | | |
| Lucy | Thou double bass and I a violin— | 35 |
| | How shall we then orchestrally unite? | |
| | | |
| Arthur | If thou consent to play with the violas, | |
| | With guile, I shall among the cellos hide. | |
| | Thus shall we closer move until, at last, | |
| | We make the sweetest music side by side. | 40 |

*[The door-bell rings.*

| | | |
|---|---|---:|
| Lucy | The clanging of percussion fills the air | |
| | Before its cue. Dear Arthur, rest thy measures— | |
| | I shall dispose of this bell-ringer promptly, | |
| | That we may soon continue our duet. | |
| | | |
| Arthur | I shall await thee, Lucy, even as | 45 |
| | Staff paper waits on notes to make it live. | |

*[Lucy leaves the drawing room, shutting the door on Arthur. She walks to the*
*vestibule and opens the front door.*

*Enter JOHN SEWARD.*

Lucy     Fair greetings, Doctor Seward.

Seward       —Miss Westenra.
'Twas most delightful to encounter thee
Along the street where, with thy mother kind,
Thou didst perambulate just yesterday.    50

Lucy     Thy conversation ever is a treat—
Direct and imperturbable art thou,
Thy work in the asylum fascinating.
*[Aside:]* In sooth, had Mina not her Jonathan,
I should think him a perfect match for her.   55
*[To Seward:]* Pray, walk aside unto the library.

*[They walk from the vestibule to the library.*

Seward    Thou profferest to me a study rare—
A study psychological, which I
With joy could spend a life unraveling.

Lucy     Am I a book that thou might read my pages?  60

Seward    Would that I might, to view the words therein,
The secret sentences of thy dear heart.
Sweet Lucy, thou hast grown most dear to me—
Consider what a life we might enjoy
As characters whose stories are combin'd.   65

Lucy

*[aside:]* Alas, this reader turns to fantasy,
A genre that my library stocks not.
Toward nonfiction must I steer his passion.
                              *[The door-bell rings.*
That must be Mister Morris at the door—
He said he would arrive at half past three,          70
Yet whilst I spoke with Arthur and with John
I quite forgot the third who was expected.
*[To Seward:]* Pray, sit, and in the library remain.
Be thou a worthy reader, and tread not
Within the drawing room that lies beyond.            75
A minor character is at the door—
Some merchant or a flower girl, belike—
Yet we our chapter shall conclude anon.


Seward

My patience could contain whole paragraphs.


*[She leaves Seward in the library and walks to the vestibule.*


*Enter QUINCEY MORRIS at the door.*


Lucy

O, Mister Morris, thou hast made it four.            80


Morris

Nay, nay, three thirty, as we did agree.
Some words of import I'd discuss with thee—
May we step further into thy fair house?


Lucy

*[aside:]* The drawing room and library are fill'd
With his two rivals—I must keep him here!            85
*[To Morris:]* Thy riding-boots, dear Quincey, grasp
                                        the mud
To which my family estate is prone.
Think me not rude if I propose we talk
Within the vestibule.

Morris      —It suits me well,
And even as thou dost propose we talk,    90
I shall talk of proposals presently.
Miss Lucy, I know I'm a simple man,
Not good enow to tie your riding shoes,
Yet if thou waitest on a better man
Thou mayst be waiting till the judgment day.   95
Why not hitch up thy wagon next to mine,
And we shall ride the road of life together,
A double harness t'ward the setting sun?

Lucy      Good Quincey, thou art passionate and kind,
A noble man of moral, upright bearing.    100
Some lucky lass shall join her carriage to
Thy wagon and be fortunate withal.

Morris     I hear thy meaning, though thou shoot'st not straight.

Seward     *[aside:]* I hear a voice that doth disrupt my tale.

Arthur     *[aside:]* I hear the beating of my drum-like heart.   105

Morris     Thou art an honest-hearted lass, I know—
Clean grit unto the depths of thy sweet soul.
Tell me, though, as a friend unto another:
Dost thy heart, Lucy, long for someone else?
Tell me and, if there is, I swear I ne'er    110
Shall trouble thee a hair's breadth more,
Yet shall remain, to thee, a faithful friend.

Lucy      Indeed, my hopes are firmly fasten'd to
Another coach, which captur'd all my love
Ere thou didst e'en arrive unto the ranch,    115
Though I confess the other coachman hath
Not yet announc'd his love for this poor rider.

                *[Aside:]* Why should not women be allow'd to wed
                Three husbands, thus to save the world from hurt?

Morris        My brave, brave lass. 'Twas better worth t'arrive     120
                Late for a chance of winning thy pure hand
                Than driving hard for any other girl.
                If th'other fellow knoweth what is well,
                He shall pursue the road ahead with strength
                Or answer unto me. Thy honesty           125
                Hast made me friend, far rarer than a lover,
                Less selfish too. Now I must make the walk—
                The lonely walk twixt here and kingdom come.
                                    *[Lucy kisses him on the cheek.*
                By this fond kiss thou mak'st me thine fore'er,
                A loyal friend unto the end. Farewell.        130

                                    *[Exit Morris.*

Lucy          *[aside:]* This noble carriage teaches me myself,
                For I'd not realiz'd what my heart desir'd
                Till Quincey offer'd me his rope and hitch.

                                *[Lucy returns to the library.*

Arthur        *[aside:]* Good lady, when may our next movement start?

Seward        Good lady, our next chapter may begin.        135

Lucy          In which, belike, our wagons must detach.

Seward        Why words of wagons whilst I wag o'er words?

Lucy          *[aside:]* There are as many metaphors as men—
                Where is the hunter who could track them all?
                Shall I become Diana, they the stags?       140

One more! Like rampant weeds do they arise!

| | |
|---|---|
| Seward | To speak plain volumes in a single phrase: |
| | I'd talk of marriage, not of carriages. |

Lucy      Pray, John, be thou an author sensible     145
And waste not words on unreceptive eyes.

Seward    'Tis not thine eyes I hope shall scan my suit—
Thy heart is my preferrèd readership.

Lucy      Unto another's shelves my heart hath turn'd,
There to receive the poetry of love.     150

Seward    Thy words are clear, thy sentences most plain.
Couldst thou, in time, come to adore my pen?
Long would I wait for such an epilogue.

Lucy      Nay, John. Thou art a man of virtue and
Intelligence, yet not my future mate.     155

Seward    I have been—and shall always be—thy friend;
Thine answer most direct ensures it so.
If e'er thou shouldst a true companion need,
Thou must count me among the best. Adieu.

*[Exit Seward.*

Lucy      Two gallant, fair proposals in one hour,     160
Whist he who singeth music to my heart
Hath not yet tun'd his instrument to love.
Back to him, for the long-awaited coda.

*[Lucy returns to the drawing room.*

Arthur          Sweet Lucy, my baton hath lain too still
                Whilst—so fear I—another one conducts          165
                The masterpiece of thine affections.

Lucy                            —Nay,
                Be not misled: I keep no other beat,
                None shall conduct my heartstrings but myself.

Arthur          True, dear, thou art a proud, pois'd soloist.
                Yet there is one who longs to play beside         170
                Thee long as life and music shall endure.
                I love thee past all metaphors and symbols,
                I love thee and shall love thee evermore,
                I love thee wholly, Lucy Westenra,
                I love thee, light abundant, lucid luck,          175
                I love thee truly—wilt thou marry me?

Lucy            Thou, Arthur, tell'st me all I long'd to hear.
                I am thy Lucy, true until death parts us.

                                    *[They kiss and remain on stage.*

                    *Enter MINA MURRAY on balcony.*

Mina            Sweet Lucy, I receiv'd thy wondrous news—
                A suitor, a proposal, an engagement!              180
                My heart bursts for thy happiness profound.
                Would that my Jonathan could hear the tale;
                Since his last letter, none have I receiv'd—
                I hope there is no matter with the man
                That keepeth him from sending word to me.         185
                I wonder where he is—would he were here,
                His joy for Arthur and thyself would be
                Surpass'd but by mine own. O, can it be?
                How is it fortune smileth on us, that

We found the best of husbands, best of men?    190
I see, as I toward the future gaze,
The promise of the merriest of days.

*[Exeunt.*

## SCENE 2.
### *London. An asylum.*

*Enter JOHN SEWARD.*

Seward    My suit rebuff'd at Lucy's charming hand,
Today I find an emptiness within.
I have no appetite, my mind is fog—
The only cure shall be a day of work.
One patient doth afford much interest,    5
Whom I have question'd more than others, thus
To understand his deep hallucinations.
Troth, I would keep him at the point of madness,
Which I avoid with other patients as
I would avoid the very mouth of hell.    10
His name is R.M. Renfield: strength profound,
A sanguine temper'ment, yet morbidly
Excitable with periods of gloom.
His appetite, unlike mine own that ebbs,
Runs rampant, though for most unusual tastes.    15
I'll see him now, rejection to forget.

*Enter R.M. RENFIELD, searching throughout his cell .*

Renfield    O, Doctor Seward, you gave me a shock.
I was but—tidying, yea, tidying,
To give my room a sheen and nothing more.

| | | |
|---|---|---|
| Seward | Thou wert not searching for another fly | 20 |
| | To make thy supper, as hath been thy wont? | |
| | | |
| Renfield | A fly? Nay, I confess, I eat no flies. | |

*[A spider crawls across the floor. Renfield picks it up and eats it.*

| | | |
|---|---|---|
| Seward | Is that a spider, Renfield, that thou eat'st? | |
| | | |
| Renfield | Is not the octopus a luxury | |
| | To those who serve and eat it on our coasts? | 25 |
| | Is not the squid a delicacy rare | |
| | To those who catch and cook it for their meals? | |
| | These octopods are culinary gems— | |
| | Hath not a spider eight legs such as these? | |
| | Why should I, then, not seek its flavor sweet? | 30 |
| | My predilection for the humble fly, | |
| | An insect crunchy, crispy on the tongue, | |
| | Is now replac'd by savory arachnids, | |
| | Which give the throat a tickle as they pass. | |
| | O, judge not, Seward, till you taste it too. | 35 |
| | | |
| Seward | Occasion that shall never come to pass. | |
| | Though I did scold thee when thou fed'st on flies, | |
| | My mind misgives at this new tendency. | |
| | What is that little box thou seem'st to hide? | |
| | | |
| Renfield | It holdeth spiders, produce of the hunt. | 40 |
| | Each one is logg'd within my notebook, sir— | |
| | Most carefully have I recorded them. | |
| | | |
| Seward | *[aside:]* The better that we may thy madness prove. | |
| | *[To Renfield:]* The box doth rattle with a movement as | |
| | Not even a tarantula could cause— | 45 |
| | Is't only spiders which thou hold'st therein? | |

Renfield  A cunning eye, good Doctor Seward, yea—
      I do confess I have a sparrow caught,
      And added it to my collection sweet.

Seward   A sparrow? O, what shalt thou do withal?   50
      Thou hast no means to cook a bird aright.

Renfield  Cook, nay. I pray, do not concern yourself.
      Yet, if you would indulge me, Doctor Seward—

Seward   What satisfaction canst thou have tonight?

Renfield  A kitten: little, sleek, and playful, too,   55
      Which I shall pet, and teach, and feed—and feed!

Seward   From flies to spiders, sparrows unto kittens—
      Belike thou wouldst enjoy a household cat?

Renfield  Yea, yea! A cat, O, I would like a cat!
      I ask'd you merely for a kitten lest   60
      You should refuse a cat. Say it may be!
      None could refuse me one small kitten, could they?

Seward   Alas, I fear it is impossible,
      Though I shall make the proper enquiries.
      *[Aside:]* I shall, of course, do no such thing as this,   65
      Lest the authorities should think me mad
      And set me in a cell beside this man.

Renfield  Please, Doctor Seward, find me but one cat—
      Troth, my salvation doth depend upon't!

Seward   One question further, then must I depart:   70
      The feathers in the corner of thy cell,

The spot of blood upon thy pillowcase—
What is the tale that I should learn from these?

Renfield   I'll say no more. You turn to mockery.

           *Exit Renfield as Seward leaves the cell.*

Seward   A case as strange as this requires new words,  75
      If I would classify him properly.
      He is no homicidal maniac;
      Precision doth demand another term.
      Zoöphagous—life-eating—maniac,
      Such is the group of which he is the first.  80
      He seeketh to absorb as many lives
      As he is able, starting from the small—
      The insects and arachnids he consumes—
      Then onto larger birds and animals.
      This need, perchance, he'll prove on cats and dogs,  85
      Then afterward up higher, I suspect.
      Where would this madness lead, if left uncheck'd?
      How large a creature would the man collect?

                *[Exit.*

## SCENE 3.

*Night. Aboard the* **Demeter**, *a ship sailing toward England.*

*Enter CAPTAIN and BOATSWAIN.*

Captain   Boatswain!

Boatswain     —Here, master: what cheer?

Captain       —What is this
      O'er which the crew doth whisper furtively?

> Their sharp dissatisfaction reaches me,
> Though I know not the content of their gloom.

Boatswain  Forsooth, I've heard the rumblings but know not.    5
                        Methinks it beareth a connection to
                        The cargo—mostly caskets—which we bear,
                        Yet wherefore this should be is still unknown.
                        Perhaps we should assemble our fine crew
                        And ask them openly about the matter?    10

Captain  A scratch neglected soon becomes infected,
                        So goes the wisdom of the mighty seas.
                        Call forth the crew, I bid thee.

Boatswain  —Presently!

*The BOATSWAIN sounds a whistle. Enter various CREW MEMBERS.*

Captain  Some strange disquiet comes o'er the *Demeter*:
                        Where there should be a harvest, I see weeds,    15
                        Where there should be fertility, naught grows,
                        Where there should be a feast, there hunger reigns.
                        Your captain doth command ye: speak the reason.

Crew 1  It is the caskets we have ta'en on board—
                        There is a certain evilness about them.    20

Crew 2  Moreover, something is aboard the ship.
                        I dare not speculate what it may be,
                        Yet we have seen it, rising from the caskets.

Crew 3  A strange shape, tall and thin, much like a man—
                        Yet not one of the crew, as I do live.    25

| | |
|---|---|
| Boatswain | Shapes, somethings, evilness—these are but fears! |
| | Your superstition and your folly do |
| | O'ersway the better wisdom of your minds. |

| | | |
|---|---|---|
| Captain | Be not so hasty, boatswain, for this crew | |
| | Hath been as loyal as a riding donkey. | 30 |
| | Are they not our crew faithful, whom we two | |
| | Have ridden with until this very day? | |
| | And were they ever wont to act this way? | |

| | |
|---|---|
| Boatswain | Nay, truly. |

| | | |
|---|---|---|
| Captain |             —Let us make a search complete: | |
| | From stem to stern, let no jot stay conceal'd. | 35 |
| | Take lanterns, for the night is dark as sin. | |

| | |
|---|---|
| Crew 2 | E'en as you say, sir, so shall it be done. |

*[Exeunt crew members.*

| | | |
|---|---|---|
| Boatswain | Though years I've plied my trade upon the sea, | |
| | Ne'er heard I such a fuss about the cargo— | |
| | Yea, not since Atlas was a load so noted. | 40 |

| | |
|---|---|
| Captain | Perchance 'tis more than superstitious dread— |
| | Dost thou not feel it? Shakes it not thy bones? |
| | There seems some doom about this ship entire. |

*[Offstage, a crew member screams, and the scream is suddenly cut short.*

| | | |
|---|---|---|
| Boatswain | What is this shrill sound piercing the dull night? | |
| | Some blast of wind or call of shrieking bird? | 45 |

| | |
|---|---|
| Captain | 'Twas one of our dear crew, whose awful wails |
| | I recognize as if 'twere mine own babe. |

[Another scream.

| | | |
|---|---|---|
| Boatswain | Some nightingale, belike, whose evening call<br>Is tun'd unto the likeness of a man. | |
| | | |
| Captain | Thy fears do render thy poor ears dishonest— | 50 |
| | Thou knowest 'tis the crying of our crew. | |
| | What creature is it we have borne with us? | |
| | What fiend of hell makes brave crew members yelp? | |
| | O England, thy great shores come not too soon. | |

Enter CREW MEMBER 3.

| | | |
|---|---|---|
| Crew 3 | 'Tis here! I know it, captain, I have seen't! | 55 |
| | 'Tis ghastly pale, all stretch'd and gaunt and vile. | |
| | 'Twas in the bows and fell upon our men. | |
| | My knife I wielded, creeping up behind, | |
| | And slash'd with all the strength of my right arm, | |
| | Yet 'twas as vapor, like the very air— | 60 |
| | The blade pass'd through it an 'twere emptiness. | |
| | | |
| Boatswain | Come, I shall go with thee, 'tis naught but fright: | |
| | Some illness or some madness coming o'er | |
| | Our noble crew, which makes ye sore afraid. | |

[Exeunt boatswain and crew member 3.

| | | |
|---|---|---|
| Captain | *[kneeling:]* Eternal one, whose heaven is above, | 65 |
| | Be with my crew in this, our hour of need. | |
| | O hear us when we cry aloud to thee, | |
| | For those in peril on the untam'd sea. | |

Another scream offstage. Enter BOATSWAIN.

Boatswain       O save me, save me! Aye, the devil's here!
                This is his ship, we his unwilling crew,                70
                And hell shall prove our final destination.
                Sir, pray protect thyself ere 'tis too late!
                The sea shall save us from him—gentle sea,
                Whose waves are like a balm unto the soul,
                Whose waters blue and green have carried me,           75
                Whose tides and rhythms beat with mine own heart,
                Thou art the only prospect that remains!

                        *[Exit boatswain, leaping over the rail into the sea.*

Captain         Still fog, which even sunrise cannot pierce.
                I dare not go below or leave my helm
                To see the horror that hath ta'en my crew.            80
                My boatswain, peradventure, was correct
                To hurdle overboard and make escape,
                For better 'tis to perish in the hands
                Of our one love, the sea, than in fear cruel;
                To die a sailor in blue water is                      85
                A passing to which no one can object.
                Yet, as the captain, I must stay the course,
                I must not leave the ship, come foe or fate.
                This fiend or monster I shall baffle, though—
                Whene'er I feel my strength begin to fail,            90
                I'll fix my hands with ties unto the wheel.
                Then he—or it—shall dare not touch my frame
                Lest all the ship be sunk, the fiend withal.
                I feel myself grow weaker even now.
                The night is deep, the morn still hours away,         95
                But by God's heav'n, I may still save my soul.
                For I have many promises to keep,
                And miles to go before my final sleep.

                        *[Exit.*

# SCENE 4.

*Whitby. The shoreline.*

*Enter various CITIZENS, looking out to sea.*

Citizen 4     Behold the ship that doth approach the land,
Which knocketh strangely yon and hither both.
Its captain, so it seems, knows not his mind—
The storm he spyeth brooding in the sky,
Yet cannot figure whether to turn north     5
Or make his landing here at Whitby's pier.

Citizen 5     Foolhardiness, it seemeth, is its crew.
The other ships come unto port sans harm,
And with each safe arrival there's a cheer
From all who watch the clouds most ominous.     10
The squall's apparent to the simplest sailor,
Yet this ship rushes headlong through the gale.

Citizen 6     Its sails are set wide open, for the sea.
It floateth with such speed that it shall fetch
Up somewhere, even if 'tis but in hell.     15

Citizen 7     It cometh—O, it cometh horribly—
At Tate Hill Pier the ship shall meet its end!

*The ship appears on stage and crashes. The body of the CAPTAIN is tied
to the ship.*

Citizen 6     It splits! It breaks!

Citizen 4          —O, I have suffered
With those that I saw suffer: a brave vessel,
Who had, no doubt, some noble creature in her,     20

Dash'd all to pieces. O, the cry did knock
Against my very heart. Poor souls, they perish'd,

Citizen 5    Yet only one, it doth appear, remains—
Observe that being most unfortunate.

Citizen 7    Unto the ship at once, and we shall see.    25

*[The citizens board the ship, which is now still.*

Citizen 4    O corse unholy, tether'd to the helm.
The head doth droop, and swingeth violently
With ev'ry shifting of the massive ship.

Citizen 6    'Tis only by some miracle it hath
Made landfall e'en as safely as it did.    30
No other crew are here, far as I see—
Unsteer'd it was, save by a dead man's hand!

Citizen 7    Here comes the surgeon, to inspect the scene.

*Enter J.M. CAFFYN.*

Caffyn    Make way, I bid ye—I must see this man,
And whether there is any spark of life    35
That doth remain within his tousl'd frame.

Citizen 5    It takes no doctor to declare him dead—
I'd swear upon my life he hath expir'd.

Caffyn    Indeed, thy simple observation's true.
He hath been dead some two days, by my troth,    40
Yet for some reason tied himself thereon,
And fashion'd knots by manner of his teeth.

Citizen 4      What is that token resting in his hand?

Citizen 6      A crucifix, by heaven, with its beads
               Tied fast around his two hands and the wheel.      45

Citizen 7      What portent of some greater evil's this?

Citizen 6      Belike the man knew he was perishing,
               And sought th'almighty's help to steer him on.

Citizen 5      Methinks not since old Jonah hath there been
               Such ardent faith at sea giv'n answer full.      50

Citizen 4      Who's this that cometh now to see the ship?

Citizen 7      I know the man. 'Tis Billington who comes—
               A most esteem'd solicitor of Whitby.

                    *Enter S.F. BILLINGTON.*

Billington     This vessel have I been expecting, sirs.
               It is the schooner *Demeter*, from Russia.      55
               Despite its landing most unfortunate,
               I must consign its cargo to my firm.

Caffyn         Speak'st thou of commerce in the face of death?
               Hast thou no heart?

Billington                 —Yea, heart alongside brain.
               There's naught that can be done for this poor soul,      60
               Who did his duty, as a captain ought.
               Shall we undo his most heroic deed
               By spurning that for which he gave his life:
               The safe arrival of the load he carried?

| | | |
|---|---|---|
| Citizen 5 | *[aside:]* An argument in letters capital. | 65 |

| | |
|---|---|
| Caffyn | Have thy way, then. We'll search the ship entire, |
| | And all the cargo shall be render'd thee. |

| | |
|---|---|
| Billington | My thanks. |

| | |
|---|---|
| Citizen 4 | —What is it that the ship doth hold? |

| | | |
|---|---|---|
| Billington | A number of great wooden caskets, sirrah, | |
| | Which my unnamèd client would protect | 70 |
| | At any cost. | |

| | |
|---|---|
| Caffyn | —Come, we'll discuss the whole. |

*[Exeunt Caffyn and Billington.*

| | |
|---|---|
| Citizen 6 | This captain shall be lauded for his deeds. |
| | I'll warrant hundreds shall request to take |
| | Their final rest wheree'er his body lies. |

| | | |
|---|---|---|
| Citizen 7 | With trouble cometh trouble, more and more; | 75 |
| | I fear some evil lands on England's shore. | |

*[Exeunt.*

## SCENE 5.

*The Westenra seaside estate in Whitby. Evening.*

*Enter MINA MURRAY and LUCY WESTENRA.*

| | |
|---|---|
| Mina | How wonderful, this visit unto Whitby, |
| | For which we long have plann'd and dream'd and pin'd. |
| | We two are reunited finally: |
| | This Mina hath her Lucy. |

Lucy                    —Verily,
            And let us not take leave so long again.          5
            It must not take a journey to the north
            To bring together such strong friends as we.
            What news, dear Mina, mayst thou share with me?


Mina        Joy, joy, joy! News, at last, of Jonathan.
            He hath been gravely ill, and thus wrote not.       10
            A letter came from Sister Agatha,
            A nun who ministers to my love's health.
            In troth, she careth for two hearts at once.
            Soon I shall leave to join him—


Lucy                    —Wondrous! Where?


Mina        In Transylvania, where he doth recover.            15
            I'll be his nurse and helpmeet as requir'd,
            Then bring him home. Kind Mister Hawkins saith
            'Twould serve us well to wed in that far land,
            That our bright future knows no more delay.


Lucy        O Mina—tidings most miraculous!                    20
            A truly blessèd end to thy concern,
            Which hath these many weeks—nay, months—been
                                              thine.


Mina        My spirit overflows with gratitude.
            And what of thy life, Lucy, canst thou tell?
            Mak'st thou the preparations to wed Arthur?         25


Lucy        Within the month, I hope it may occur.
            He is the gentlest man I ever met,
            And seeketh ever for my ease and care.

Mina        No less than thou abundantly deserv'st.

Lucy        One wrinkle mars the fabric of our lives—        30
            A trifle, yet a thing I must unfold
            Ere we go to our slumber presently.
            Of late, sleepwalking is become my wont:
            I have been seen to fully dress myself,
            Or amble o'er the grounds unconsciously.        35
            No memory of these nocturnal sprees
            Have I once I awake, but just the sense
            Of having pass'd a peaceful, pleasant night.

                        *[They change into bedclothes.*

Mina        How strange, my dear. I hope all shall be well.

Lucy        Good Doctor Seward says this stage shall pass,        40
            Yet ere we sleep, 'twas right that thou shouldst know.

Mina        Good-night, then, Lucy. Deep may thy sleep be.

Lucy        With thou beside me, Mina, I've no fear.

                        *[They sleep. Exit Lucy, unseen.*

Mina        *[dreaming:]* Ho, Jonathan! Pray, leave me not in fear!
            *[Waking:]* Alas, I have been dreaming all this while.        45
            The night is dark—dear Lucy, art thou there?
                        *[Mina lights a candle.*
            O, wherefore art thou absent from thy bed?
            What spirit calls thee forth from slumbering?
            Thank heav'n, her dressing-gown and dress remain—
            She, therefore, cannot be too far afield.        50
            The door unto the terrace is ajar;
            I'll take a shawl and thither search for her.

[Mina steps into the terrace.

The moon is bright and full, the clouds dark gray,
A fleeting landscape twixt both light and shade.
There, far away, upon the eastern cliff,      55
I spy the abbey ruins we explor'd
More times than I can count in years gone by—
Its church and graveyard barely visible.


*Enter LUCY WESTENRA, seated, in the graveyard. Enter DRACULA,
behind her. Both are in the fog and difficult to see.
MINA seems them distantly.*


There—there she is! Upon our fav'rite seat!
A touch of white within the night most grim,      60
A glimpse of light to touch a world gone dark,
A drop of snow upon a sea of black,
Which may, with slightest provocation, melt.
Yet what is that, which creepeth near her back—
A man? A beast? A phantom of the night?      65
If but the clouds would part and let the moon
Shine forth with all her power luminous—
Then could I see what apparition comes.
It bendeth o'er her, yet she moveth not.
I'll haste me to her, fleet as feet may fly!      70
O Lucy, Lucy, fear not—I approach!

[Mina runs toward Lucy.

The creature turns its eyes to look at me—
How red they gleam, despite the frightful dark.
Be gone, thou beast! Disturb not Lucy's rest!
The clouds come o'er the moon; full dark again!      75

[Exit Dracula. Mina reaches Lucy.

My Lucy safe, and quite alone at last.
The being, whether physical or spectral,
Hath fled, and my dear friend is safe at last.

Lucy        *[waking:]* Brave Mina, is it thee? My body quakes—
            I am as cold as ever I have been.                           80
            'Twas not a dream, for it seem'd all too real.
            My only thought was coming to this place—
            I know not why, or what it was I fear'd.
            Though I did slumber, I recall my journey—
            The terrace door, the garden, and the cliff.                85
            It seems I heard the howls of many dogs,
            The whole town fill'd with curs who bray'd like sirens.
            Within my recollection I can see
            A creature, long and dark, with eyes of red.
            'Twas somehow sweet and bitter both at once—                90
            My soul did from my body take its leave
            And float about the air, an 'twere a ghost.
            An agonizing feeling shook me, then,
            Like mighty earthquake rocking all the world.
            'Twas then I woke and found thee shaking me—                95
            I saw thee do it, Mina, ere I felt it.

Mina        Come, Lucy, we shall have thee home anon,
            Where I shall wash thy feet and tuck thee in,
            And we shall whisper pray'rs of thankfulness
            For God's protection giv'n to thee tonight.                 100
            Pray, take this shawl, which I shall fasten on thee.


                        *[Mina clasps the shawl around Lucy's neck.*

Lucy        Pray, Mina, speak to no one of this night—
            My mother and my father must not know,
            For they shall only worry o'er my health.

Mina        Come, Lucy, think not on them till the morn.                105
            Inside, I bid thee, let us quickly walk.
            *[Aside:]* What are these pricks of blood upon her
                                                        nightdress?

Belike I stuck her with a pin as I
Secur'd the shawl around her pallid neck.
'Tis this and nothing more, I do expect—                110
Now swiftly in, with steps and course direct.


*[Exeunt.*


## SCENE 6.
### *London. An asylum.*


*Enter JOHN SEWARD and R.M. RENFIELD.*


Renfield    Nay, Doctor Seward, press me not to speak—
I would not talk with thee; thy station's naught,
For even now the master is at hand.
The traveler will come in chosen form,
And many folk shall soon know what 'tis to                5
Be toss'd and roasted in the depths of hell.


Seward    *[aside:]* His madness turneth t'ward divinity,
Where he is angel to a mighty god.
*[To Renfield:]* What of thine animals which thou
               collect'st?
Find'st thou no joy in thy menagerie?                10


Renfield    Bother them all! I nothing care for them.


Seward    No care for flies or spiders? Even birds?


Renfield    Much joy there is unto the eyes that view
The maidens waiting for the bride to come,
Yet when the bride arriveth, eyes are fill'd,                15
And have no time for silly maidens' games.

Seward         *[aside:]* He looks no longer at me, but peers out—
               The window of his little cell doth face
               Th'estate of Carfax, which he gazes on
               As if it were the holiest cathedral,                    20
               Where God's real presence waits for Renfield's tongue
               In holy—or unholy—eucharist.


Renfield       I'm here to do your bidding, master, yea—
               I am your servant, whom you shall reward,
               For I am ever faithful to your call.                    25
               Long have I worshipp'd you, and from afar,
               Yet now that you draw near, I wait on you.
               Your virtuous commands shall prove delights.
               O, do not pass me by when you arrive,
               Remember me as you give all good things                 30
               To those who truly know and wait on you.
               My veins are pulsating like battle drums—
               I shall be patient, master. O, he comes!


                                                          *[Exeunt.*

# ACT III

# SCENE 1.
### *The hospital of Saint Joseph, Buda-pesth.*

*Enter MINA MURRAY and SISTER AGATHA.*

Mina

Dear Sister Agatha, you have my thanks
For taking in my weary Jonathan.
Please, tell me how he fareth in your care.

Agatha

He came to us plagu'd by brain fever harsh,
And hath for some six weeks been resting here.          5
In his delirium, his ravings hath
Been dreadful, rife with poison'd brews and blood,
With ghosts and demons and such horrid beasts.
The ravings of the sick are secrets of
Almighty God, which I shall not repeat.          10
I only tell you that I may say this:
Excite him not too much, I bid ye, madam.

*Enter JONATHAN HARKER.*

Mina

*[aside:]* My true love cometh, yet how diff'rent he:
So thin and pale, so weak where he was strong,
All resolution wanting from his eyes,          15
His quiet dignity quite vanishèd.

Jonathan

Sweet Mina, thou hast come to me at last.

Mina

Dear Jonathan, forgive my long delay.
Far too much time hast thou without me pass'd,
Yet 'twas but recently I knew the way:          20
We heard about thy solitude of late,
And on the instant eastward was I bound.

Jonathan        I know, my love, that thou wouldst never wait
To rush unto my side with care profound.

Mina        How cam'st thou here? Does thou remember aught?  25

Jonathan        Alas, I've tried, but nothing can recall.
Methinks I was within some foul net caught,
And only barely fled a violent squall.

Mina        Kind Sister, can you tell us nothing of
The words he spoke when hither he arriv'd?  30
Would they not give some clue to his ordeal?

Agatha        Be sure, 'twas nothing to concern your mind—
No wrong that he committed was confess'd,
And he remembers you and your devotion.
His fear was of things great and terrible,  35
Which mortal understanding cannot treat.

Jonathan        Pray, Agatha, deliver me my coat,
Whose contents I shall show my bride to be.
*[Agatha hands Jonathan his coat.*
O Wilhelmina, harsh life's antidote,
Hear thou these words with great solemnity:  40
Thou knowest 'tis my vehement belief
That—twixt two folk whose souls are bound as one—
A secret, kept conceal'd, brings both to grief;
'Tis honesty through which true love is won.
When I think on the trials I have fac'd,  45
My head doth spin and I bethink me mad.
*[Jonathan pulls a notebook from the coat, offering it to Mina.*
Yet, in this notebook is the truth encas'd,
Which daily did I further pages add.
I would not know the horrors it doth hold,
But would prefer pure ignorance and bliss.  50

Read if thou wish'st, but let me not be told—
Seal thou this promise with a holy kiss.

> *[Mina and Jonathan kiss.*

Let us be wed, ere comes another night.
Kind Sister Agatha gives her consent.

Mina    Thou art my future and my fond delight,    55
And as thy wife shall I e'er be content.

Agatha    By dispensation of the holy church,
I may perform the rite for you at once.
Will you, Jonathan Harker, ever be
A true and faithful spouse to this dear woman?    60

Jonathan    I will, so help me heaven.

Mina    *[aside:]* —Ah, my love,
Who speaks the words in voice so firm and strong!

Agatha    Will you, then, Wilhelmina Murray, be
A true and faithful spouse to this dear man?

Mina    I will, so help me heav'n.

Jonathan    *[aside:]* —My life! My joy!    65

Agatha    Then, by the might of the almighty one
Who join'd our ancestors in Eden pure,
I call you wife and husband, bound fore'er.
What God hath join'd, let no one put asunder.

Mina    I take thy hand the first time as thy wife,    70
The happy ending I have long desir'd.

Jonathan      I would endure more challenges or strife
              To win thy love again, were it requir'd.

Agatha         Come, let us feast and toast your married life
              Ere homeward ye depart with health acquir'd.        75

*[Exeunt.*

## SCENE 2.

### *London. An asylum.*

*Enter JOHN SEWARD and ARTHUR HOLMWOOD.*

Arthur        My thanks for seeing Lucy after her
              Sleepwalking episode of yesternight.
              Canst tell me, John, what thou discoverèdst?

Seward       In friendship and the wish of happiness
              I came to Lucy and thyself, good fellow.          5
              She was more pale and bloodless than before,
              Yet of anemic signs I nothing saw.
              Her blood, which I examin'd carefully,
              Shows naught but health and vigor by its hue
              And composition.

Arthur                   —Thus far, then, all's well.        10
              What dost thou think the problem, then, can be?
              Canst thou, like clever kitten, find the rat?

Seward       Belike the problem lieth in her mind—
              She doth complain of breathing trouble and
              Of heavy and lethargic slumber, too,         15
              Which comes with dreams that fright her horribly,
              Yet which she can remember not a whit.

Arthur          What remedy then John, for, by thy look,
                I see thou hast not given up all hope.

Seward          Unto my friend and former teacher have          20
                I writ: Professor Abraham Van Helsing,
                Of Amsterdam, who knoweth more about
                Diseases strange and abstract than all others—
                His wisdom I would trust past all the world's.
                I told him of our splendid Lucy and          25
                That thou art her fiancé and true love.

Arthur          John, thou art the most trustworthy of friends.
                If this Van Helsing is as wondrous skill'd
                As thou reportest, all's well that ends well.

Seward          I am both proud and happy to provide          30
                Whatever help to Lucy and thyself
                As I may proffer. Troth, Van Helsing is
                Philosopher and metaphysician,
                Who practiceth the sciences advanc'd—
                His mind is open as the wide, wide sea,          35
                His nerve like steel that fashioneth a ship,
                His temper like the ice through which one steers,
                His kindness like the wind that fills the sails.

Arthur          We are indebted to thee utterly.

Seward          Nay, Arthur, 'tis no more than I would ask          40
                Were thou the doctor, I sweet Lucy's love.

Arthur          I shall return to her and share the news.
                How shalt thou spend the evening?

Seward                          —Visiting
                A patient whose odd case confounds me still.

Arthur        Best wishes, then, until we meet again.        45

Seward        Soon shall I, with Van Helsing, join you two,
Like magi bearing gifts of health for her.
And so, farewell. Give Lucy all my love.

Arthur        *[aside:]* She knoweth she already doth possess't.

        *[Exit Arthur.*

Seward        Back, now, to Renfield, he who hath become        50
Both my professional obsession and
Distraction from the tempest of my heart.

        *[Seward walks to Renfield's cell.*

*Enter R.M. RENFIELD, with his back turned, eating flies.*

Renfield        Each morsel is a pleasure for the lips,
Each morsel is a scratch upon the wall,
Where I shall mark how many buzzing pests        55
Become my dinner and sustain my life.

Seward        Say, Renfield, art thou at thy feast again,
Thy diet falling back, once more, to flies?

Renfield        *[turning, shocked:]* O, Doctor Seward! Wherefore dost
        thou vex
Me when I long to have my privacy?        60
Apologies—I have, of late, regress'd,
For all is lost. He hath deserted me!
No hope remaineth for my soul unless
I seize my fate and unto action turn!
Wilt thou some sugar bring, I beg thee, sir?        65

Seward          For these thy flies?

Renfield                    —They long for its sweet taste.

Seward          I shall indulge thee, Renfield, this last time.

*[Seward turns to leave and Renfield pulls a knife from his pocket,*
*preparing to attack.*

Renfield        My master, I shall come to thee anon!
                Bless my endeavors, all perform'd for you!

*[Renfield swipes at Seward, cutting his wrist and causing it to bleed.*
*Seward overcomes Renfield and takes the knife.*

Seward          What is this madness? How hast thou that knife?          70
                Attendants, come! Pray, I have been attack'd!

*Enter two ATTENDANTS, who seize RENFIELD and*
*hold him to the floor.*

Attendant 1     What happen'd, Doctor Seward? Are you well?
                He had the knife! And did he cut you, sir?

Seward          A touch, a touch, I do confess.

Attendant 2                  —You bleed?

Seward          A little, yea, yet not too badly harm'd.          75

Attendant 1     Behold the patient!

Attendant 2                  —Licketh he the ground?

Seward       *[aside:]* 'Tis where the few red beads of my blood fell.
             He slurpeth them as if he were a dog
             That thirsts and laps the smallest water droplets.

Renfield     The blood is life! The blood is life profound!          80
             The blood is life, pour'd freshly on the ground!

*[Exeunt.*

## SCENE 3.

*The Westenra home, London.*

*Enter ABRAHAM VAN HELSING, holding a medical bag.*

Van Helsing  Sent for by Seward, patient of my past,
             Unto this city—London—have I come,
             Now to examine the unhappy lass
             Long suffering from dream-fill'd, sleepless nights.
             In Seward's letter found I sev'ral clues—          5
             God help us if they point t'ward what I think,
             Help anyone who faceth such a fate,
             Troth, help the needful 'gainst a mighty foe.

*He enters the bedchamber. Enter LUCY WESTENRA, in bed, and*
*ARTHUR HOLMWOOD, seated beside her.*

Lucy         You are Van Helsing, or I am mistook.
             Most welcome to our humble fam'ly home.          10

Arthur       Dear sir, we are most grateful you are come.

Van Helsing  No need have we of these formalities,
             For we three shall soon prove the best of friends,
             Against the worst of enemies—ill health.

| | |
|---|---|
| Lucy | *[aside:]* It seem'd he would some baser rival name,    15<br>But stopp'd himself lest it give us a fright. |

*Enter JOHN SEWARD.*

| | |
|---|---|
| Seward | Van Helsing! |
| Van Helsing |       —Seward. Now are we all met. |
| Seward | My carriage hither somewhat was delay'd—<br>Apologies if ye have waited long. |
| Van Helsing | Like tortoise 'fore the hare did I arrive;    20<br>Mere seconds after me thou hither com'st,<br>But long enow for me to meet these two.<br>*[To Lucy:]* My dear young miss, 'tis well to know thee, for<br>I know how much thou art belov'd by all. |
| Lucy | 'Tis gentleness in thee to speak so well.    25 |
| Van Helsing | If thou shalt place thyself within my hands,<br>I'd make a full examination, lass. |
| Lucy | E'en as thou sayest, doctor, it shall be. |

*[Van Helsing examines Lucy while Arthur and Seward speak.*

| | |
|---|---|
| Seward | How fares young Lucy, Arthur? |
| Arthur |       —She is pale,<br>And hath but little energy to spare.    30 |
| Seward | Such was my fear. Since last I saw the lass,<br>Her face is gaunt, the red gone from her cheek. |

*[Van Helsing rejoins them.*

| | | |
|---|---|---|
| Van Helsing | There is no time, or all is surely lost— | |
| | She'll die for want of blood if she doth not | |
| | Receive a swift transfusion of the same. | 35 |
| | Shall it be me? | |

Seward       —I am the younger, sir.

Arthur       Jack, stand apart and call a stalwart arm.

*[Arthur opens his sleeve.*

Van Helsing       Thou art the lover of our dear, dear miss,
Who suffereth most gravely—courage now!
Thou canst do more than anyone alive.     40

Arthur       My soul for hers, my last drop for her life.

Van Helsing       Her empty veins are pining for a drink.
John would have giv'n his own, but thine is best—
Our nerves are not so calm as thy nerves are,
Our blood is not so bright as thy blood is.     45

*[They pull equipment from Van Helsing's bag.*

Arthur       One love's kiss, first: so sweet was ne'er so fatal.

*[Arthur kisses Lucy.*

Van Helsing       *[aside to Seward:]* He is so young and strong, with blood
so pure,
That we need not defibrinate the source.

| | | |
|---|---|---|
| Seward | Now all is ready. Come, the instruments. | |
| Van Helsing | Take thou this draught, sweet lady, to prepare. | 50 |
| Seward | I'll help her drink—prepare ye Arthur's veins. | |

*[They attach needles and tubes to Arthur and Lucy.*

| | | |
|---|---|---|
| Van Helsing | Come, blood, that is the very source of health. | |
| | Come, blood, that pulseth in each human vein. | |
| | Come, blood, perform thy vitalizing work, | |
| | Come, blood, and save the life of this poor lass. | 55 |
| Seward | See how, already, blush comes to her face, | |
| | A quickening so swift I ne'er beheld. | |
| Arthur | I feel myself grow wan with effort rare, | |
| | Yet never felt such joy as now, when I | |
| | Espy the vigor coming back to her. | 60 |
| Lucy | *[waking:]* Help me, dear Arthur, help me! Do thy best | |
| | To pluck this crawling serpent from my breast! | |
| | Ay me, for pity! What a dream was here! | |
| Arthur | My dear, my Lucy! | |
| Lucy | —Arthur, what befalls? | |
| Van Helsing | He shares a gift most precious with his love, | 65 |
| | For even now the man doth bleed for thee. | |
| Seward | Rest, Lucy. To thy slumber make return. | |
| Lucy | I am afeard. | |

Seward                    —Of going back to sleep?
          Such is the boon that ev'ry person craves

Lucy          Not if they did endure what sleep brings me:          70
          It is a presage of a horror worse.

Van Helsing   What meanest thou? I bid thee, plainly say.

Lucy          I know not, for 'tis more than words can speak.
          Not knowing is where terror, partly, lies—
          This weakness cometh to me in my sleep          75
          Such that I dread the very thought of it.

Arthur        Tonight thou may in perfect quiet rest.
          We shall watch o'er thee ev'ry second, dear.

Seward        If we should witness any evidence
          Of foul dreams plaguing thee, we'll wake thee swiftly. 80

Lucy          O, will ye truly? You are angels three,
          And neath your ministrations I may sleep.

*[She closes her eyes and sleeps. Seward and Van Helsing step aside.*

Seward        Brave Arthur, by the rings upon thine eyes
          I see that rest hath been denied thee much.
          Let the professor and myself keep watch,          85
          That thou mayst sleep while she's a-slumber, too.

Arthur        Your kindness doth exceed what we deserve.

Seward        Nay, not a whit. 'Tis done in friendship's name.

Arthur        Then I, with friendship, do receive the kindness,
          And with my thanks depart unto my bed.          90

*[Exit Arthur.*

Van Helsing     What mak'st thou of the marks upon her neck?

Seward     Upon her neck? I'd not examin'd them.

Van Helsing     Her symptoms, which by letter thou describ'st,
Of sev'ral foul diseases did remind me.
Long did I pore o'er books of ev'ry sort—     95
Yea, I prepar'd an 'twere a wager grave,
Which fate did set, with Lucy's life at stake—
And through my studies rose one likelihood,
The symptoms pointing t'ward an awful end.
Each mark upon her neck confirms the thought.     100
Remain here while I fetch my larger trunk.

Seward     Without the giving of thy diagnosis?
O, wilt thou leave me so unsatisfied?

Van Helsing     Should I prove right, thou shalt know all anon.

*[Exit Van Helsing. A fog appears in the room.*

Seward     Though I must stay awake, for sleep I long—     105
My eyelids shut like they were weighted down,
And sleep comes o'er me as a fun'ral shroud.
Forgive, kind Lucy, for thy watchman fades—

*SEWARD sleeps. Enter DRACULA, barely seen in the mist.*
*DRACULA leans over LUCY for some moments, then departs.*
*Enter ABRAHAM VAN HELSING, setting down his trunk.*

Van Helsing     O, Gott in Himmel!

Seward            —What? Was I asleep?

Van Helsing       The lass! Look to the poor and weary lass!        110

Seward            Dear Lucy, paler than she was before—
                  Her lips like alabaster, gums shrunk back,
                  As if she were already corse become.

Van Helsing       'Tis not too late. Her heart doth feebly beat.
                  Our work's undone; we must begin anew.          115
                  Young Arthur hath already given much
                  And is not here to open up his veins.
                  It must be thou, John—let us recommence.

                  *[Van Helsing attaches needles and tubes to Seward and Lucy.*

Seward            I know not what o'ercame me suddenly—
                  The urge to sleep was not to be denied.         120
                  'Twas like dark magic render'd me inert.

Van Helsing       Belike thou hittest closer to the mark
                  Than thou imaginest. Be still and quiet—
                  Let us not wake her whilst she blood receives.

Seward            Now blood, flow on—O honor, to do good.         125

Van Helsing       Meanwhile, I shall unveil my fragrant gift.

                  *[He opens his trunk and pulls out flowers.*

Seward            What are these flowers, odorous and white?

Van Helsing       I shall explain unto ye both at once.
                  The color doth return to Lucy's cheek—
                  Come, we shall end this unforeseen transfusion.   130

Seward	Art certain? Thou took'st more of Arthur's blood.

Van Helsing	He is her lover, her fiancé, and
His only purpose is to live for her.
Thou hast much work to do for her and others—
We need thee strong for all the toil to come.	135

Seward	E'en as thou sayest.

Van Helsing	—No word speak of this
Emergency transfusion unto Arthur—
He would be both parts jealous and afraid.

*[Van Helsing removes the tubes and wakes Lucy.*

Lucy	How many hours have I in slumber lain?
I see the sun arising in the east,	140
And feel the strength of two men in my bones.

Seward	Thou slept more than we hop'd, less than thou need'st.

Lucy	We owe thee so much, Doctor Seward—John—
For all thou undertakest for my health,
Yet thou must never overwork thyself.	145
How pale thou seemest. By my troth, thou need'st
A wife and nurse to minister to thee.

Seward	*[aside:]* If but she knew how these words sting my soul.

Van Helsing	These flowers I brought here for thee, Miss Lucy.

Lucy	For me? Professor, what a dear thou art.	150

Van Helsing	They are not merely for beholding, though:

They are medicinal.

Lucy                 —Must I eat them?
Already doth their pungency o'erwhelm
The passageways of my nose delicate.

Van Helsing   Not to ingest, nay, but to tolerate:       155
Their smell, though strong, thou must attempt to bear.
I'll place them in thy window, on thy tables,
Enwrap a wreath around thy gentle neck.

*[Van Helsing hands Lucy a flower and she smells it.*

Lucy       Thou art in jest—thou com'st from Amsterdam
To ply thy tricks upon a helpless lady.      160
This is but common garlic, nothing more!

Van Helsing   Nay, trifle not with me—I never jest.
In all I do there is a purpose grim,
And I warn all of ye 'gainst thwarting it.
Mistake me not, my dear, and fear me none:    165
I swear, there's virtue much in these sharp flow'rs.
John, help me, that we may the room adorn.

*[Van Helsing and Seward remove garlic from the trunk, placing it around*
*the chamber.*

Seward     No pharmacopoeia is known to me
That calleth for such potent smells as this.
I trust Van Helsing, though, with mine own life—   170
And, Lucy, what is more, with thy life too.
Professor, ever hast thou reasons for
Thine actions, which appear bewildering.
A skeptic might declare thou work'st a spell
Or try to keep out evil spirits. Ha!       175

Van Helsing    Perhaps 'tis so. *[To Lucy:]* Take care not to disturb
The garlic, and thy windows open not.
The door, too, must both clos'd and lock'd remain
Except when Arthur, John, or I must enter.

Lucy    I promise it shall be as thou dost say.    180
A thousand thanks for thine attentiveness.
How have I such kindhearted friends deserv'd?

Van Helsing    Rest now, and we shall come to thee again.

Seward    *[aside:]* What doth this mean? My life among the mad
Begins, I'll warrant, to affect my mind.    185

*[Exeunt Van Helsing and Seward.*

Lucy    How good and dutiful are they to me.
John Seward proves himself a friend sincere,
Devoted to my comfort and recov'ry.
Van Helsing is a tender, clever man—
At first his fierceness was a fright to me,    190
Yet now his wisdom shineth like the dawn:
Already I feel comfort from the flow'rs
And somehow do not dread the thought of sleep.
The pain and fear of slumber dissipates,
Which these past weeks hath plagu'd me terribly.    195
How bless'd are they who know no cause for dread,
Whose lives are free of sorrow or concern,
Who think of sleep but as their nightly blessing
That bringeth naught but dreams both sweet and calm.
Before today, I lik'd not garlic well;    200
Now find I peace and solace in its smell.

*[Exit.*

## SCENE 4.
### *Exeter.*

### Enter *MINA HARKER, JONATHAN HARKER,*
### *and PETER HAWKINS.*

Hawkins      Dear friends, ye heartily are welcome back
From your adventures—mayhap misadventures—
In Transylvania. With great joy have I
Observ'd you as you grew from children to
The wonderful adults before mine eyes.      5
Pray, share my dwelling and, when I am gone—
As I have neither chick nor child at all—
Take ev'rything I own, with all my love.
*[Aside:]* This is, in some part, recompense for guilt,
For Dracula did give me such a fright      10
That I foresaw much trouble in the task—
Thus Jonathan I sent, to take my place!

Jonathan      Such greeting, sir, as ne'er did I expect!

Mina      An offer that we never could repay.

Hawkins      Nor shall ye. Tell me, Mina, and be true:      15
How is the health of thy brave Jonathan,
Who shall become full partner in our firm?

Mina      I tell thee truly, Peter: he is still
Much weaken'd by his serious ordeal,
Yet is rebuilding flesh upon those bones.      20
He sometimes waketh trembling in the night,
Until I coax him to placidity.

| Hawkins | Then Theseus is still within the maze, |
| | The minotaur of ill-health chasing him. |

| Mina | E'en so. |

| Jonathan | —Thy gifts, dear Peter, help me heal. | 25 |
| | Thou art more generous than one whose child |
| | Doth want a glass of water and receives |
| | A sea entire. |

| Hawkins | —No more than is thy due. |
| | Come ye within, and we shall raise a flagon |
| | Unto the fortune life hath given me, | 30 |
| | Unto the fortune that shall soon be yours. |

*[Exeunt Hawkins and Jonathan.*

| Mina | Our joy is near complete, if only I |
| | Might hear some news of Lucy and her illness. |
| | Her letter last was troubling in its news— |
| | More struggles, one step forward, one step back. | 35 |
| | I dare not ask of fate a further boon, |
| | Except that I would see my friend whole soon. |

*[Exit.*

## SCENE 5.

*The Westenra home, London. Night, then day.*

*Enter LUCY WESTENRA.*

| Lucy | Repulsive have the nights once more become, |
| | The fear they once held rising like the moon |
| | That sheds its pale and fearful light above |
| | A graveyard where the dead begin to stir. |

Forbidding are these images, yet they 5
Are with me, whether sleeping or awake.
Van Helsing, John, and Arthur are away,
Desiring their own rest whilst I take mine,
These flowers my protection in their stead.
Yet I can feel the flowers' magic fading, 10
Its potency not what it was before.
How I wish I could sleep, yet would not sleep—
My paranoia leads to paradox.

*[A sound.*

Is anybody there? Who draweth nigh?
Beyond the window taketh form a shape: 15
A bat, but of such size as ne'er I saw,
A wolf, with fangs bar'd, ready for the kill,
A shadow that suggesteth human form—
What are these shapes of horror and disgust?
To bed at once—O, let this be a dream! 20

*[Exit.*

*Daylight. Enter ARTHUR HOLMWOOD, JOHN SEWARD, and
ABRAHAM VAN HELSING, outside the WESTENRA home.*

Seward          But are the windows and the doors all lock'd?

Arthur          Barr'd utterly, as if to keep out foes.

Van Helsing     Or keep out friends, that beasts may roam within
                And ply their evil unreservedly.

Arthur          Think'st thou 'tis so?

Van Helsing                —We know not till we enter. 25
                I fear we come too late—God's will be done!

Seward   Hast thou, professor, implements within
         Thy sack with which we may our entry force?

*[Van Helsing pulls saws and knives from his medical bag.*

Van Helsing   Whate'er looks sharpest unto your sharp eyes,
              Seize quickly on't! Here's a knocking indeed!        30
              Knock, knock, who's there? We shall turn porters three!

*[They cut through the window into Lucy's chamber.*

*Enter LUCY WESTENRA, in bed.*

Arthur   O, Lucy, weaker than she e'er hath been!
         Behold the whiteness of her luscious cheek—
         Doth it foretell a most untimely end?

Van Helsing   What shall we do? Where may we turn for help?        35
              We three are spent from toil too strenuous,
              For we already gave our blood for her
              As oft as she requir'd, yet now she doth
              Another swift transfusion need, else her
              Poor life shall not be worth an hour's expense.        40
              How shall we find an open vein for her?

*Enter QUINCEY MORRIS.*

Morris   How shall mine serve—wilt find me strong enow?

Seward   What—Quincey Morris! What hath brought thee
                                                    hither?

Morris   A message sent by Arthur days ago,
         Requesting that I come to Lucy's aid.        45
         Those simple words were motivation plenty

To bring me unto London in a trice.
It seems I have arriv'd in perfect time—
Instruct me how I may be of some use.

*[They make preparation for a transfusion.*

| | | |
|---|---|---:|
| Van Helsing | Draw up thy sleeve—thine arm shall be the source! | 50 |
| | Ebbs now her life, yet thou mayst save her still. | |
| | Courageous blood is hardiest of all | |
| | And 'tis exactly what our Lucy needs. | |
| | Perchance the devil counters us himself— | |
| | Invoking pow'rs of hell to keep her weak | 55 |
| | That he might drag another soul below. | |
| | Angelic throngs surround her, though, in strength; | |
| | Thy coming is unquestionable proof. | |
| | I bid thee, bleed as thou ne'er bledst before, | |
| | Ope fully and completely unto her, | 60 |
| | Ne'er faltering in gallantry and vigor. | |
| Morris | Brisk, blessèd benefits befall brave blood. | |
| Arthur | Thou comest, Quincey, in the perfect time. | |
| Morris | Jack Seward, I seek not to interrupt | |
| | The bus'ness of thy care medicinal, | 65 |
| | Yet clearly 'tis no ordinary case. | |
| | When I appear'd, 'twas said that Lucy must | |
| | Receive transfusion further, meaning she | |
| | Already hath ta'en blood as she doth now? | |
| Seward | Indeed, 'tis so. | |
| Morris | —And the professor and | 70 |
| | Thyself did ope your veins as I have done? | |

Seward          Thou hast it right—and Arthur ere we two.

Morris          'Twas my conjecture. *[To Arthur:]* When I saw thee last,
                Thou look'd as drawn as e'er I saw a man.
                Once did I see a mare that had been bit                    75
                By those large bats which they do "vampires" call.
                The flying beast attack'd her in the night
                And drank its fill of blood from her strong frame.
                She could not even stand, she was so spent,
                And out of mercy did I end her life.                       80
                How long hath Lucy needed blood like this?

Arthur          Some ten days now.

Morris                        —Ten days! With three strong men
                Assisting in the filling of her veins?
                What illness or disease hath ta'en it out?

Seward          Such is the crux whereon doth rest her case.              85

                *[Van Helsing removes the tubes from Lucy and Morris.*

Van Helsing     I am afeard. This last transfusion hath
                Not put the color back in Lucy's visage.

Arthur          Alack!

Seward                        —The lady cannot rally. O,
                Poor Lucy, darling of our fourfold hearts.

Morris          Behold, her face grows paler, nearly white,               90
                More like a statue than a woman's skin.

Arthur          Behold, her aspect turns more beautiful—
                Methinks she groweth younger suddenly.

Van Helsing  Behold, her snowy teeth increase in length,
The canines longer, sharper than the rest.                    95

Seward  Behold, her neck by miracle is cur'd—
The two wounds vanish'd that long fester'd there.

Van Helsing  *[to Arthur:]* She dieth, Arthur. 'Twill not be long now.

Arthur  My Lucy, love on whom I pinn'd my hopes,
Shalt thou be taken from me evermore?                    100
By heaven, would that I were in thy place,
To take the suffering that thou hast borne,
To put myself in peril for thy sake.
How pitiful, how dreadful is this end.

Lucy  *[waking:]* Thou camest, Arthur—thou art by my side. 105

*[Arthur begins to kiss Lucy.*

Van Helsing  Nay, hold her hand—more comfort shall it give.

Seward  E'en as we watch, the transformation comes—
Yet no death rattle as I e'er beheld.
She groweth lovelier with each weak breath,
Her teeth the sharper, like a lioness.                    110

Lucy  Kiss me but one time, Arthur, ere I go.
The sweetest lips await a final touch.

*[Arthur begins to kiss Lucy again, and Van Helsing pushes him out of the way.*

Van Helsing  Not for thy life, thy living soul, and hers!

*[Lucy's face changes from rage to calm.*

Lucy  Thou art a friend most true, professor, yea.
    Pray, guard my Arthur's life and give me peace.  115

Van Helsing I swear I shall perform what must be done.
    Come, Arthur, there is safety presently:
    Take thou her hand, and place a kiss upon
    The lady's forehead—once—for memory.

       *[Arthur kisses Lucy on the forehead. Her eyes close.*

Lucy  Commend me to my kind Lord: O, farewell!  120

               *[Lucy dies.*

Morris  'Tis over; she is gone.

Arthur     —Breaks now my heart.

Morris  Come with me, Arthur. Let us share our grief.

       *[Exeunt Morris and Arthur arm in arm.*

Seward  Death gives her back her beauty mockingly—
    Her brow and cheeks regain their flowing lines,
    Her rosy lips have lost their deadly pallor.  125
    Our Lucy—there is peace for her at last.

Van Helsing The way she died shall set the whole world spinning.
    This is no end, John—'tis but the beginning.

             *[Exeunt.*

# ACT IV

# SCENE 1.

### *London. A street.*

*Enter MINA HARKER and JONATHAN HARKER.*

Mina

This visit unto Piccadilly may,
Methinks, give comfort to our grieving hearts.
For Mister Hawkins in his grave doth lay,
Who hath supported thee in all thy parts—
Past all our hopes—thou art a partner now,     5
The business thine, our fortune bounteous.


Jonathan

His generosity to us, somehow,
Was unexpected as 'twas plenteous.
Dear Mina—wife!—by his beneficence
Our future's safe; as if he were a god     10
Who blesses mortals with munificence.
Hold thou my hand and we shall promenade.


Mina

A life of teaching etiquette to maids
Shall I o'ercome to take thy hand in mine
And publicly display love that not fades,     15
But groweth e'en as eight turns into nine.


*Enter DRACULA across the street, but not seeing them.*

Jonathan

Zounds! Not in London! May it never be!
How cometh that foul monster to our city?


Mina

What is it, Jonathan? Whom dost thou see?
That man across the street with face so gritty—     20
His beaky nose and beard are sharpest black,
His aspect is unkind, his teeth are long,
His lips shine redder than the butcher's rack.
Why starest thou at him with fear so strong?

Jonathan     Dost thou not recognize the man insane?    25
Of course, thou couldst not know—thou wast not there.
It is the man himself!

Mina       —Be thou more plain.

Jonathan     It is Count Dracula at whom I stare.

*[Exit Dracula.*
'Tis surely he, yet he hath younger grown.
My God, if this be so! What can it mean?    30

Mina       *[aside:]* Hath my poor Jonathan his senses flown?
*[Aloud:]* Art sure 'twas that same man whom we have
seen?
*[Jonathan faints.*
Why fall'st thou, Jonathan? Ah fate, just when
The cup of happiness is at our lips.
Shall that moon envious arise again,    35
The sun of our contentment to eclipse?

Jonathan     *[waking:]* Why Mina, did I swiftly fall asleep?
Forgive me, darling—how surpassing rude!
Come, let us to our happy amble keep,
Perchance we'll have a teatime interlude.    40

Mina       *[aside:]* He hath forgotten quite the stranger tall,
Whose very aspect gave him such a fright.
His memories do cause his mind to stall,
And keeps the past beneath a shroud of night.

*Enter MESSENGER.*

Messenger    Forgive me, madam, are you Mina Harker,    45
And this man Mister Harker?

Mina                    —Verily.

Messenger               Your valet told me where you may be found,
                        And how I should your garments recognize.

Jonathan                What is the matter?

Messenger                        —I've a letter, sir,
                        Which is for Missus Mina to review.                    50

*[The messenger hands a letter to Mina. Jonathan hands the messenger a coin.*

Jonathan                My thanks for your persistence in your toil.
                        Go with our thanks and these few ducats, sirrah.

                                                        *[Exit messenger.*

Mina                    What news is it that comes so swiftly on?
                        *[Reading:]* "Thou shalt be griev'd to hear the news I tell:
                        Our dearest Lucy yesterday hath gone—                    55
                        In troth, she died, and thus in woe I dwell.
                        Come ye with Jonathan to visit soon,
                        And we shall tell you all." So Arthur writes.
                        Alas, my Lucy! Sings my heart a tune
                        Of misery and funereal rites.                    60

Jonathan                E'en on the instant when we settl'd were—
                        Why turneth foul what once was passing fair?

Mina                    *[aside:]* Of Jonathan's health, too, now so unsure!
                        God help us that we may our troubles bear.

                                                        *[Exeunt.*

# SCENE 2.

### *The Westenra home, London.*

*Enter ABRAHAM VAN HELSING, standing in front of*
*LUCY WESTENRA's body.*

| | | |
|---|---|---|
| Van Helsing | So much of grief, so little time to mourn. | |
| | This Miss Westenra was a pretty lass, | |
| | And won the heart of ev'ry man she met— | |
| | Know her and love her, so the maxim goes. | |
| | Earth doth not cease its motion, though, for death, | 5 |
| | Though we might wish more time for reverence, | |
| | Hours pass and our belov'd departed ones | |
| | Remain within death's endless, cold embrace. | |
| | O, would that Lucy fully were at rest! | |
| | Unless we further, drastic measures take— | 10 |
| | Grant her the sleep unending she deserves— | |
| | Her death shall prove a menace unrestrain'd | |
| | To haunt the English isle forevermore. | |
| | How to enlighten John of what we must | |
| | Endeavor to accomplish for our sakes, | 15 |
| | Her sake, the sake of our eternal souls? | |
| | Extraordinary my proposal shall | |
| | Appear unto his doctor's mind, I'll wager— | |
| | Reply unto his arguments I must, | |
| | That we may stop the evil ere it spreads. | 20 |

*Enter JOHN SEWARD.*

| | |
|---|---|
| Seward | Professor, Morris said thou call'dst for me? |
| Van Helsing | Hast thou brought hither thy post-mortem knives? |
| Seward | Think'st thou we need an autopsy complete? |

Van Helsing My thorny answer is both yea and nay.
I wish to operate, this much is true,  25
Yet not as thou imaginest I shall.
Let me explain as simply as I may:
I would cut off her head, take out her heart.

Seward What? Nay, sir!

Van Helsing   —Thou a surgeon, yet so shock'd?
How many times have I seen thee perform  30
Such operations with a steady hand
As would make other people faint and shudder?
We must go to the lady's coffin soon,
Lest any evil should proliferate.

Seward Yet wherefore should we so? The lass is dead.  35
Why mutilate her body sans the need?
There is no good to her, to us, to science,
To human understanding—wherefore, then?
Without such reasons, monstrous is the act.

Van Helsing Friend John, I pity thy poor bleeding heart,  40
And love thee more because it doth so bleed.
There are full many things thou knowest not,
But that you shall know in the course of time—
And render me much thanks that I did know,
Though they, assurèdly, are dreadful things.  45
We two are friends and colleagues many years:
Have e'er I taken action sans a cause?

Seward Nay, sir, 'tis very true.

Van Helsing   —And was it not
For such that thou didst send for me to come,
When trouble past all measure rear'd its head?  50

| | |
|---|---|
| Seward | Indeed, for I believ'd thou wouldst know best. |

| | | |
|---|---|---|
| Van Helsing | I know how shock'd thou wert when I refus'd | |
| | To grant that Arthur give his love one kiss | |
| | Ere she did shuffle off her mortal coil, | |
| | Yet didst thou hear the voice with which she thank'd | |
| | me? | 55 |

| | |
|---|---|
| Seward | I mark'd it well—its beauty and its grace. |

| | |
|---|---|
| Van Helsing | Trust, then, that I have purpose for my plan. |

| | |
|---|---|
| Seward | Yet wherefore must we so? What is the need? |

| | | |
|---|---|---|
| Van Helsing | Nay, reason not the need till thou know'st more. | |
| | Believe me yet a little while, friend John. | 60 |
| | There are still days more terrible to come— | |
| | Let us not be two souls, but one united, | |
| | That we may work together to good ends. | |

*Enter ARTHUR HOLMWOOD and QUINCEY MORRIS.*

| | | |
|---|---|---|
| Arthur | We come to visit Lucy where she rests. | |
| | Ah, no! I cannot bear the sight of her, | 65 |
| | Unnaturally stiff and still and cold. | |

| | |
|---|---|
| Morris | Poor fellow, thou art under such a strain. |

| | |
|---|---|
| Arthur | What shall I do? The whole of life seems gone, |
| | With nothing left that's worth the living for. |

| | | |
|---|---|---|
| Seward | Come, look upon the one whom thou call'dst love. | 70 |

Arthur        How beautiful she looks, how clear of skin,
              'Tis like she never tasted death's dull feast.
              Pray tell me, Seward—is she truly dead?

Seward        She is, I promise thee. There is no doubt.
              *[Aside:]* Yet even as I say these soothing words,        75
              The lie in them comes quickly to the fore—
              Ne'er saw I life so obvious in death,
              Ne'er saw I corse that look'd like it might wake,
              Shake off its sleep, stand up, and carry on.

Van Helsing   Pray, Lord Godalming—

Arthur                        —Arthur, please, professor.        80
              Thou show'd such kindness to my Lucy, which
              She understood e'en better than myself.
              If I was boorish or unkind to thee
              Upon the hour of her untimely death,
              I beg thee, in thy goodness, to forgive.        85

Van Helsing   I know 'twas hard for thee to trust me then,
              And still you may not trust me utterly.
              The time must surely come, however, when
              Thy trust in me shall be complete and whole,
              And all shall be reveal'd at last, as though        90
              The sun itself came beaming through the clouds.

Arthur        In ev'rything I shall trust thee, professor.
              Thou hast a noble heart and art Jack's friend,
              And most of all thou wert a friend to Lucy.

Van Helsing   Permit me, in the presence of these men,        95
              To make request of thee.

Arthur                        —Ask anything.

| | |
|---|---|
| Van Helsing | Thy Lucy left to thee, her fiancé, |
| | Her every possession. |

| | |
|---|---|
| Arthur | —Well I wot. |

Van Helsing     Thy papers and her letters would I read,
An thou shalt give me leave. I'll keep them safe    100
And render them to thee when I have done.

Arthur     Pray, Abraham, do all that thou desir'st,
And tell us what discoveries thou mak'st.
In Hampstead shall we bury my sweet lass,
To bring her peace, though peace is gone fore'er.    105
If we may find some reason for her death,
'Tis worth our thought, our toil, our strength, our breath.

*[Exeunt.*

## SCENE 3.

*The Harker home, London.*

*Enter MINA HARKER and JONATHAN HARKER.*

Mina     Th'arrival of Van Helsing comes anon—
He hath read Lucy's journals, notes, and letters.

Jonathan     Think'st thou there shall new understanding dawn,
That may release my spirit from its fetters?

Mina     He speculates your cases share a link,    5
Which may on thine experience shed light.

Jonathan     I shall consider well what he doth think
Should it help set mine anxious mind aright.

*A knock at the door. Enter ABRAHAM VAN HELSING.*

Van Helsing     Miss Murray, is it not?

Mina                  —Now Missus Harker.
Professor Abraham Van Helsing?

Van Helsing            —Yea.            10

Jonathan     Thou art most welcome.

Van Helsing          —Thank you, Mister Harker.

Mina         We are the sheep and thou the shepherd, sir:
We'll gladly follow whither thou shalt lead.

Van Helsing    You were so good to send your writings, both
The record kept by Jonathan when he      15
Was captive in the castle of the Count,
And Mina's journal of the visit to
Miss Lucy, and her vexing sleepwalking.
These chronicles, which quickly I perus'd,
Did prove themselves invaluable to me.      20

Jonathan     What mak'st thou of the odd accounts therein?

Van Helsing    Thy tale is strange and terrible—but true.
Each thing thou saw'st at Castle Dracula
Occur'd e'en as thou sayest, I believe.

Jonathan     Thy words are solace unexpected, sir.      25
How many times these last months have I fear'd
That what methought I underwent was madness!
I knew not if I could my mem'ries trust,

And since have liv'd life on the razor's edge
Betwixt reality and senselessness.                          30

Van Helsing    Be not afeard—thou sanest art of men.
*[To Mina:]* And thou a gift of heaven, by my troth,
Not only for thy love to Jonathan,
But for the careful records that thou keep'st.
I could not ask a better secretary.                          35

Mina           I only hope it shall advance our cause.

Jonathan       Tell me, I prithee: do thine enquiries
Concern the Count?

Van Helsing            —They do, undoubtedly.

Jonathan       Then I am with thee heart and soul.

Mina                   —Forsooth!
Thou ask'd us to prepare the recent news,                    40
Writ down in the relations; they are here.

*[Van Helsing peers over the papers.*

Van Helsing    Mein Gott! So soon—I did not think 'twould be!

*[Mina looks at the paper with him.*

Mina           *[reads:]* "A mystery in Hampstead doth arise.
Young children, lately, playing on the Heath,
Have seen a figure walking o'er the green.                   45
They speak about a 'bloofer lady' who
Doth beckon children, leading them astray.
Most oft late in the evening this occureth,
And twice the children were not seen till morn.

Some seem to bear small marks upon their throats,  50
Suggesting rats or dogs have gnaw'd at them
Whilst they their 'bloofer lady' pastime ply.
'Tis harmless, yet the constables of Hampstead
Are on the watch for children wandering."
Doth this strange tale have aught to do with us?  55
Why dost thy face, professor, turn so pale?

Van Helsing  It must be done, or other souls shall fall.
It must be done; the readiness is all.

*[Exeunt.*

## SCENE 4.

*Hampstead. A graveyard.*

*Enter JOHN SEWARD.*

Seward  The day comes on apace when we must do—
I dare not speak the too-unnerving words,
To say what we must do, think on the act.
Tonight Van Helsing bids us meet with him
To undertake such heresies on Lucy—  5
Nay nay, I can no more. To merely say't
Is too perverse, much less to do the deed.

*Enter ABRAHAM VAN HELSING.*

Van Helsing  Art ready, Seward, for what we shall do?

Seward  Nay, I am not, and never shall be so.

*Enter ARTHUR HOLMWOOD and QUINCEY MORRIS.*

Arthur            We are all met. Your call was plain enow,            10
                  And at th'appointed time have we appear'd
                  The place, however, warrants explanation:
                  Why are we at the mausoleum where
                  My Lucy's body is foree'er interr'd?

Van Helsing       I shall explain, and you shall see anon.            15
                  Know ye the rumors that excite all Hampstead,
                  About the 'bloofer lady'?

Morris                         —What of that?

Van Helsing       The whispers of strange punctures on the neck—
                  Two holes with blood that dot the children's throats.

Seward            Thou drawest some connection unto Lucy,            20
                  Who also had two holes upon her neck?
                  Thou dost, I'll wager, postulate this theory:
                  Whatever injur'd her hath injur'd them.

Van Helsing       Thou ever wert a student quick to learn,
                  But thy words are but indirectly true.             25

Arthur            Hast thou determin'd then, how she did die?

Seward            'Twas nervous failure caus'd by loss of blood.

Morris            How could it be that she did lose so much?

Van Helsing       Already dost thou have the answer, Morris,
                  For thou didst mention it when first thou cam'st.   30
                  The bats that, in the southern regions, come
                  And drink the blood of horses and of cattle—
                  Which even have been known to suck the veins
                  Of soldiers sleeping on a passing ship,

|  |  |  |
|---|---|---|
|  | Who woke upon the morn as white as snow, | 35 |
|  | E'en as our Lucy was when she expir'd. |  |

Arthur      Good God, a bat? In London, dost thou think?
E'en in a modern era like our own?

Seward      Thou leadest us upon a goose chase, sir.

Van Helsing      Nay, Seward: I ask only your belief.      40
Believe in things ye cannot, for my sake.

Morris      How should we so?

Van Helsing      *[to Seward:]*      —Think'st thou the small holes in
The children's throats came by the selfsame beast
As bit our Lucy?

Seward      —Yea, it must be thus.

Van Helsing      Yet thou art wrong. O, would that it were so!      45
Alas, 'tis worse. 'Tis far, far worse, I fear.

Arthur      What dost thou mean, professor? Be direct!

Van Helsing      The children's holes were by Miss Lucy made.

Seward      Good sir, thou speakest with a madman's tongue!

Morris      How darest thou make such insinuation!      50

Van Helsing      Let us unto the coffin and behold.
I swear my words shall not prove baseless tales.

*[They approach Lucy's coffin.*

Arthur          What must we do?

Van Helsing              —Let us the lid remove.

Arthur          Art thou in earnest, or is this a jest?
                Professor, I have given thee my trust,                55
                As I did swear. But shouldst thou forfeit it,
                I shall proclaim thy lunacy abroad.

Van Helsing     Thou warnest me e'en as a lover should.
                If I could even one pang spare thee, friend,
                God knoweth that I would. Yet, sir, this night        60
                Our feet must tread in thorny paths or else
                The feet thou lov'st must walk in paths of flame.
                If Lucy's dead, there's naught can wrong her now.
                Yet if she is not dead—

Morris                   —What meaneth this?
                Think'st thou she lives?

Van Helsing              —I did not say alive.                        65
                I merely say that she may be undead.

Arthur          Undead? Is this some nightmare whilst we wake?

Van Helsing     Pray, let us ope the coffin. Ye shall see.

Arthur          Professor, being that I flow in grief,
                The smallest twine may lead me. As thou wilt.         70

                        *[They remove the lid of the coffin. It is empty.*

Van Helsing     Are ye not satisfied, good sirs? What say ye?

Seward          I am but satisfied her body doth
                Not lie within the coffin, yet the fact
                Proves but one thing.

Van Helsing                —And what is that, friend John?

Seward          That 'tis not there.

Van Helsing                —Thy logic's dull but sound.          75
                How shall we three give reason for its absence?

Morris          Perchance a body-snatcher? May it be?

Van Helsing     Come, come, you answer with an idle tongue.

Morris          Go, go, you question with a wickèd tongue.

Van Helsing     Remember how she did appear at death?          80

Arthur          More beautiful than ever I have seen.

Morris          She blushèd red, although she wanted blood.

Seward          Her teeth did seem to grow and sharpen quite.

Van Helsing     Hear now the answers ye seek urgently:
                Miss Lucy was within her trance-like state—          85
                Sleep-walking—when a vampire bit her neck.
                'Twas when she slept that he took so much blood.
                He forc'd sleep on thee, Seward, so that he
                Could steal to Lucy and imbibe again.
                'Tis she who haunteth Hampstead ev'ry night:          90
                Inheriting the thirst of that dread beast
                That drank of her, she sips from children's necks.

> In trance she died, and now doth live undead.
> She must be given true rest, final rest.

Arthur      How shall we do this awful, bloody work?      95

Van Helsing      There is a duty grave to be done here.

Arthur      If it be aught that doth concern my faith
            Or pers'nal honor, I can make no promise.

Van Helsing      Thy limitation, Arthur, I accept.
                 If any act of mine thou wouldst condemn,      100
                 Judge thou of whether it doth violate
                 These reservations thou hast specified.

Arthur      'Tis only fair.

Seward      *[aside:]* —Now come the hated words,
            Which once Van Helsing spake to me alone.

Van Helsing      May I cut off the head of dead Miss Lucy?      105

Arthur      By heav'n and earth, a million million nos!
            Not for the world entire shall I allow
            The mutilation of her body pure.

*Enter LUCY WESTENRA, undead, carrying a CHILD.*

Van Helsing      *[aside:]* They did believe me not; her they'll believe.

Arthur      My Lucy walking, as in life she walk'd,      110
            Yet on her is the look of foulest death.
            Her sweetness turn'd to heartless cruelty,
            Her purity to lustful wantonness,

Her lips stain'd crimson with the hue of blood,
Her eyes stare vacantly, sans sense or purpose.    115

Seward    *[aside:]* How swift my love for her turns into loathing—
I'd gladly slay her, and with wild delight.

*[Lucy drops the child to the ground.*

Morris    How carelessly she drops the helpless child,
As if it were an empty vessel now,
For which she had no further use or care.    120

Van Helsing    She doth not, truly. It hath serv'd its turn,
And given her the blood whereon she sups.

Lucy    Come to me, Arthur, leave these others now.
My arms are hungry for thee—husband, come!

*[Van Helsing holds a crucifix toward Lucy. She steps toward the coffin.*

Van Helsing    Speak, Arthur, answer me with purpose firm:    125
Shall I proceed with what I have propos'd?

Arthur    Yea—do thy will, professor, do thy will.
No horror like this horror may exist;
It is against the very plan of heav'n.

Morris    Is't truly Lucy's body that we see,    130
Or but a demon taking Lucy's shape?

Van Helsing    It is her body, yet it is not she.
Be patient; we shall see her as she was.
*[Lucy lies in the coffin.*
Ere we proceed, I'll tell thee what I know,
Which cometh from experience and lore    135

Of ancients who have studied the undead.
When such as they are form'd, the change comes with
The frightful curse of immortality.
They cannot die, but live on age to age
To add new victims to their grisly number                    140
And multiply the evils of the world.
The circle widens, like the ripples from
A stone thrown in the water carelessly.
Hadst thou, friend Arthur, met her bidding kiss
Thou wouldst have—on thy death—turn'd nosferatu. 145
So all of eastern Europe calls th'undead.
Our lady's most unfortunate career
Hath just begun. If she lives on, undead,
The children—not as yet so much the worse—
Shall lose their blood and come to be like her.              150
Yet, if she dies in truth, then all shall cease:
The wounds on those young throats shall disappear,
And our sweet Lucy shall as true dead rest,
Her soul forever set at liberty.
'Twill be a blessèd hand that sets her free.                 155
I stand most willing to perform the deed,
But who among us hath the better right?
Methinks 'twill bring thee, Arthur, passing joy
To think hereafter in night's solitude:
"'Twas I who sent her to the waiting stars,                  160
The hand of him who lov'd her first and best,
The hand she would have chosen, could she choose."

Arthur              My true friend, with a broken heart I thank thee.
                    Tell me what I must do; I'll falter not.

Van Helsing         Brave lad! A moment's courage and 'tis done.        165
                        *[Van Helsing produces a wooden stake and a hammer.*
                    This stake thou must drive cleanly through her heart.
                    'Twill fearful be—be not deceiv'd in that—

Yet shall be brief, and then mayst thou rejoice.
From this grim tomb thou shalt emerge as if
Upon the clouds thou walk'dst, with steps of light.     170
Thy friends surround thee and we pray for thee.

*[Van Helsing hands the tools to Arthur.*

Arthur          My left hand holds the stake that pierceth her,
My right hand holds the hammer that shall drive it.
*[Arthur stands over Lucy.*
With all my might, with all my love, I strike.

*[Arthur pounds the stake into Lucy's heart.*

Morris          O fount of blood that springeth from her corse,     175
O heavy deed, and yet he wavers not!

Seward          See how she writhes and twists, with stabbing screams,
See how her teeth bite down upon her lips!

Van Helsing     Behold, she stills—he pierceth through the heart.
Behold her calm; the deed at last is done.     180

Arthur          Her face, it hath return'd to its old self,
Her sweetness and her purity shine through.

Van Helsing     I hope thy full forgiveness I have earn'd.

Arthur          God bless thee for restoring her bless'd soul.

Van Helsing     If thou wouldst kiss her, now thou safely mayst—     185
Kiss thou her lips as she would have thee do,
For she is not a grinning devil now:
She is God's true dead, her soul now in heav'n.

[Arthur kisses Lucy.

Morris          What further must we do?

Van Helsing              —Take Arthur home,
                And Seward and myself shall stay to do          190
                The final ministrations to her body.
                Our first step have we taken, yet there's more:
                We must find out the author of our woe
                And stamp him out as if he were a spark.
                Some clues we have, to help us in our task,     195
                Which shall prove arduous and perilous.
                What say ye—shall ye help me do our duty?
                Shall we fight him until the bitter end?

Arthur          Through danger, death, disaster, or dismay,
                I speak for all of us when I say: yea.           200

[Exeunt.

# ACT V

# SCENE 1.
### *London. An asylum. Day.*

*Enter MINA HARKER.*

Mina      The evil now enwrapping our environs
Must be entrapp'd before it doth enlarge—
Enter th'exhilirating final act.
The caskets that, at Whitby, landfall made,
Are th'object of the first investigation      5
Myself and Jonathan have underta'en.
Good Mister Billington of Whitby did
Provide our search with papers critical
Concerning the consignment of the boxes.
These papers turn'd poor Jonathan quite pale,      10
For he had seen the selfsame messages
Within the castle of the dreaded Count,
Not knowing his schemes diabolical.
His plan, with mathematical precision,
Was to each jot and tittle well design'd.      15
With cunning had he obstacles foreseen,
Arranging all so to avoid the snares.
The cargo was thus harmlessly describ'd:
"Some fifty cases fill'd with common earth,
For mix'd experimental purposes."      20
From Whitby unto London were they sent,
All fifty boxes from the *Demeter*
Are safely stow'd at Carfax, we are told,
Though on the morrow we shall search the grounds.
Thus far doth our pursuit of him extend,      25
Until with stronger allies we unite.
Here I'll see one—John Seward—he who was
So close to Lucy in her parting days.

*Enter JOHN SEWARD.*

| | |
|---|---|
| Seward | Dear Mina, hither hast thou come at last. |
| | My thanks for meeting me in such a place. 30 |
| | |
| Mina | Now am I in th'asylum; th'more fool I. |
| | Long have I hop'd to meet thee, Doctor Seward, |
| | For thy kind actions recommend thyself— |
| | Thou didst attend on Lucy at the end, |
| | With gentleness and tenderness profound. 35 |
| | For all I know of her, I'm ever grateful; |
| | The lass was very, very dear to me. |
| | Pray, wilt thou tell me how sweet Lucy died? |
| | |
| Seward | Tell thee how she did die? Not for the world. |
| | |
| Mina | Yet wherefore not? |
| | |
| Seward | —Thine ears I'd not abuse— 40 |
| | Thy virtue not besmirch—by telling tales |
| | Which are most horrible! Naught could persuade me. |
| | |
| Mina | Mine intuition, like a speeding arrow, |
| | Hath hit the mark toward which it doth aim. |
| | Thou hast confirm'd her death was terrible. 45 |
| | Hast thou my papers read, and Jonathan's, |
| | Which we unto Van Helsing did deliver? |
| | |
| Seward | I have indeed; thou hast endur'd ordeals. |
| | |
| Mina | Thou knowest, then, that I am on thy side. |
| | If we this monster somehow may defeat, 50 |
| | No secrets must exist betwixt we two. |
| | Like hapless English standing 'gainst the French, |
| | We few, we happy few, must face this foe. |

| | | |
|---|---|---|
| Seward | My keen professor is prov'd right again: | |
| | Thou art a woman most extraordinary. | 55 |
| | Apologies, I soon shall tell thee all, | |
| | That we our forces may combine in one. | |
| | | |
| Mina | Then shall I, for Van Helsing's sake, compose | |
| | A chronological, complete account. | |
| | | |
| Seward | Ere that time comes, I fain would understand | 60 |
| | Why thou desir'dst to travel hitherward— | |
| | To the asylum—which most folk, in troth, | |
| | Would happily avoid and visit ne'er. | |
| | | |
| Mina | Van Helsing told me of thy patient—Renfield— | |
| | Whose case doth fascinate my probing mind. | 65 |
| | If thou shalt let me, I would see the man. | |
| | | |
| Seward | My pledge of loyalty to thee shall be | |
| | Applied upon the instant. Let us go, | |
| | And thou shalt meet the troubl'd, curious soul. | |
| | | |
| Mina | Thy kindness thou abundantly dost prove. | 70 |

*They walk through the asylum. Enter R.M. RENFIELD in his cell.*

| | | |
|---|---|---|
| Seward | What ho, Renfield! Thou hast a visitor— | |
| | A gentlelady comes to call on thee. | |
| | | |
| Renfield | Why should she so? | |
| | | |
| Seward |       —Th'asylum she surveys, | |
| | And would observe its many residents. | |
| | | |
| Renfield | Allow me time to tidy ere she enters. | 75 |

*[Renfield lifts his box and holds it to his mouth.*

Seward       *[aside:]* The foulest method known of tidying—
             He merely munches all the flies and spiders
             That he possesses in his little box.
             Were this the normal way of cleaning rooms,
             Methinks all England should dishevel'd be.          80

*[Renfield motions for Mina to enter.*

Mina         Good evening, Mister Renfield. I know thee,
             For Doctor Seward told me of thy case.

Renfield     Art thou the lass the Doctor wish'd to wed?
             Nay, nay, thou canst not be, for she is dead.

Mina         I have a husband, wedded ere I met          85
             Kind Doctor Seward. I am Missus Harker.

Renfield     Why hast thou come?

Seward                   —How didst—how couldst—thou know
             That 'twas my wish to marry anyone?

Renfield     A question most absurd.

Mina                     —Wherefore is't so?

Renfield     When one is priz'd and honor'd, like thy host,          90
             The whole community doth speak of him.
             Yea, Doctor Seward is belov'd by all—
             Not just his household, friends, and family,
             But by his patients, too, who—in divers,
             Odd states of mental equilibrium—          95
             Are apt to muddle causes and effects.

Seward    *[aside:]* Doth my pet lunatic converse withal
          Precision, like a polish'd gentleman?
          Perchance 'tis Missus Harker's presence that
          Doth strike some chord within his memory,          100
          As if she were a sorc'rer, this her pow'r.

Renfield  E'en I did, once, fall under a belief
          Most strange, which did alarm my caring friends.
          Yea, 'twas my fancy death could be delay'd,
          And human life prolong'd indefinitely,             105
          Should one consume a mass of living things,
          No matter how low on creation's scale.
          Neath this misguided notion did I try
          To harm our Doctor Seward, so to give
          My vital powers strength e'en through his blood.    110

Seward    *[aside:]* Is this the selfsame man who, presently,
          I witness'd swallowing an insect feast?
          He speaketh like a doctor, not a loon.

Mina      I hope thou art unto thy sense restor'd.

Renfield  Be thou assur'd of my recovery.                    115
          May heaven bless and keep thee, Madam Mina.
          I hope I ne'er again shall see thy face—
          At least, not in this unforgiving place.

*[Exeunt.*

## SCENE 2.
### *London. An asylum. Night.*

*Enter ABRAHAM VAN HELSING.*

| | | |
|---|---|---|
| Van Helsing | How wonderful this Madam Mina is, | |
| | Whose brain doth rival thinkers far and wide, | |
| | Whose heart doth flow with empathy and grace. | |
| | 'Twas heav'n above that fashion'd her so well, | |
| | And bless'd her with the combination rare. | 5 |
| | Still: should she, in this matter, be engag'd? | |
| | To hunt a monster is a frightful thing, | |
| | To catch a villain is a per'lous task, | |
| | Which may prove all-too perturbatious for | |
| | A person with a nature delicate. | 10 |
| | Soft you, Van Helsing, for they come anon: | |
| | The friends who will, together, slay the beast. | |

*Enter MINA HARKER, JONATHAN HARKER, JOHN SEWARD,*
*ARTHUR HOLMWOOD, and QUINCEY MORRIS.*

| | | |
|---|---|---|
| Jonathan | Good even, Quincey, John, professor too. | |
| | We are all gather'd, as we did agree. | |
| Arthur | The work before us passing dangerous. | 15 |
| Morris | Yet we stand ready for the task ahead. | |
| Mina | United, brave and strong: we are prepar'd. | |
| Van Helsing | Well met, then, gallants all. Let us begin. | |
| Seward | The guestrooms in the house of the asylum | |
| | Shall serve as our shar'd home whilst we attempt | 20 |

To stop the heinous fiend who stalks the land.
Ye are most welcome underneath this roof.

Arthur          We have perus'd the linear account
                Produc'd by Missus Harker and thyself,
                Which doth in ev'ry detail tell the tale          25
                Of Lucy, Jonathan, and this dark threat.

Morris          What is't we know about our enemy?

Van Helsing     Much research Doctor Seward and myself
                Have underta'en to comprehend this man—
                If man he may be call'd.

Mina                            —What have ye learn'd?          30

Van Helsing     First, to the question of our shar'd belief:
                Let us agree that vampires do exist,
                The fact of which we have some evidence.

Seward          If our unfortunate experience
                Were not enow, we have the records and          35
                The teachings that the past doth proffer us,
                Which plenty are to satisfy the sane.
                At first, I was a skeptic, I confess,
                But now the facts do thunder in mine ears.

Van Helsing     The nosferatu are not like the bee:          40
                They do not perish after they have stung,
                But grow e'en stronger in their evil pow'r.
                This Dracula possesseth now the strength
                Of twenty sturdy people at their prime.

Seward          He hath the divination of the dead,          45
                Whom he commandeth as a gen'ral doth

Give orders to the armies that he leads.
He is a brute, and can, within his range,
Direct the elements—the storm, the fog—
Subdue the meaner beasts unto his will—                50
The rat, the owl, the moth, the fox—

Arthur              —The bat?

Van Helsing   E'en so. He groweth or becometh small,
And vanisheth whenever he desireth.

Mina          Where, then, and how may we begin our strike?
What method can destroy so strong a foe?               55

Seward        Troth, this is much: our task most terrible,
Which would make e'en the bravest person shudder.

Jonathan      Yet if we fail this fight, he surely wins.
Where then are we? Our lives are at the stake.

Van Helsing   'Tis more than life or death, friend Jonathan.     60
Worse yet is that we may become as him:
Henceforward to be foul things of the night,
Sans heart or conscience, preying on the souls
And bodies of the people we love best,
The gates of heaven shut to us fore'er,                65
Abhorr'd by all, a blot upon God's light.
Are ye prepar'd, such wretchèd fates to face?

Mina          I answer for myself and Jonathan,
Who are determin'd to complete this work.

Morris        I am with ye.

Arthur              —And I, for Lucy's sake.               70

Van Helsing Consent to swear; I pray, swear by my sword.

             *[They swear.*

    We six are not without our ample strengths:
    We have the bow of science in our pack,
    The arrows of devotion to each other,
    A quiver fill'd with hours both day and night,  75
    And fletching that shall guide our purposes.

Seward  Beware, though, not to underestimate
    The powers that the Count possesseth, too:
    Brave Jonathan reports the Count eats not—
    Not of the food that nourishes ourselves—  80
    Hath no reflection in a looking-glass,
    Is stronger than an ordinary man,
    And may transform himself into a wolf.

Arthur  Or bat, as when my Lucy walk'd in sleep.

Morris  What words of comfort may ye offer us?  85

Van Helsing Though he can do these things, he is not free—
    He is more captive than those in the Tow'r,
    More prisoner than madman in a cell.
    He cannot go wherever he doth list;
    Although the man is not of nature born,  90
    He must obey the laws of nature still.
    Unless one of the household bids him come,
    He may not enter underneath its roof.
    His power ceases when the day begins,
    For sunlight is a lethal glow to him.  95
    Some things afflict him, robbing him of pow'r:
    A branch of roses plac'd upon his casket,
    A crucifix, a head of garlic too.

Morris   A leek perchance?

Seward      —Nay, for he loves the Welsh,
And finds their lifeblood flavorful and rich.   100

Van Helsing The fiend is mortal, though the manner of
His slaying is a Herculean task:
A sacred bullet fir'd into his chest,
Beheading, which doth bring the final rest,
A stake that's driven through his ghoulish heart— 105

Arthur   As I do know too well.

Seward      —Alas, 'tis true.

Mina    We must, then, find his casket where it lies.

Van Helsing Thou hast it, Madam Mina, perfectly.

Morris   The enquiries of Jonathan and Mina
Reveal'd that fifty caskets came from Whitby  110
To Carfax—Dracula's acquir'd estate.

Jonathan  Intelligence we further have discern'd,
For Mina and myself to Carfax went
To find the fifty whither they were sent.

Arthur   Alas the day! What learn'd you, there, of him? 115
How did it look when first ye saw the house?
What said its keepers? What make they of it?
Where is the Count? How parted ye from there?
Where are the caskets? Answer me in one word.

Mina    When first we came upon the house describ'd, 120
We instantly were satisfied they were

The lairs arrangèd by Count Dracula.
The house look'd long abandon'd, vacant quite,
The windows were encrusted with thick dust,
The shutters up, the framework black with time, 125
The painted iron mostly scal'd away,
The boards all loose, with edges raw and white.

Jonathan An accurate examination made we:
But twenty-nine of fifty caskets did
Remain within the house!

Mina —Methought I saw 130
A face that lurk'd behind the windowpanes,
Yet 'twas mere shadows dancing in the dark.

Jonathan We dar'd to enter, nervousness increasing.
The floor did writhe with movement sickening:
The place was rife with rats in hundreds, thousands. 135

Mina 'Twas then that Jonathan did call the dogs
That on the streets were roaming thereabout.
When those few mutts ran in, the rats dispers'd—
Although their numbers far outstripp'd the dogs,
They were most fearful when the hounds appear'd. 140

Van Helsing Your visit then, was laden with success:
No harm came to yourselves—the first, best good—
And ye discover'd caskets had gone missing.
More vital, though, is what you did observe:
The rats, though answ'ring to the Count's command, 145
Do not share in the power of his spirit.
For, though they came to Carfax when he call'd,
They scatter'd at the barking hounds' approach.
This Dracula hath fled for now—'tis well!
You are the queen and king, and we cry "Check!" 150

*Enter ATTENDANT 1.*

| | |
|---|---|
| Attendant 1 | Forgive me, Doctor Seward, for th'intrusion. |
| | 'Tis Renfield, sir—he fain would speak with you. |
| | He is importunate, most eagerly |
| | Insisting that you quickly come to him. |
| | I fear that, if you do not go at once, |
| | He may erupt into a violent fit. |

Van Helsing    Take me, I bid thee, John. I'd see the man.

Morris    As would I, too.

Arthur                    —I'll make the number four.

Mina    And Jonathan and I shall come as well.

*They walk through the asylum. Enter R.M. RENFIELD in his cell.*

Seward    What wilt thou, Renfield? How may I assist?

Renfield    I thank thee, Doctor, for thine advent swift.
But one request have I to make of thee:
Release me from this place and send me home.
I am recover'd, sounder than the owl:
Ask me the madman's name and I'll say, "Who?"
I see thou hast thy colleagues brought withal:
Let them, I bid thee, judge my sanity.
Who are they, please, that I may know them better?

Seward    One Arthur Holmwood—Lord Godalming now—
The Harkers, Jonathan and Mina they,
Professor Abraham Van Helsing, and
Good Quincey Morris of America.

Renfield      My Lord Godalming, I had once the honor
Of seconding thy father in his practice.
I grieve to realize that he is no more.      175
Dear Mister Morris, thou must be most proud
Of thy young land, the newfound colonies.
Kind Mina, I delight to see thee here,
And with thy husband, handsome and astute—
Thine is a tale of ardor singular.      180
Professor, O! My pleasure is profound
To have thine eminence within my cell.
Thy work hath science revolutioniz'd
By thy discoveries about the brain:
Thou art the first among a class of greats.      185

Seward      *[aside:]* But can it be? His reason is restor'd!
Shall I declare him well and send him hence?
I must be patient, for his nature is
As changeable as weather on the sea.
*[Aloud:]* Thou art improving rapidly, I see.      190
Upon the morn we may discuss this further.

Renfield      I fear thou hardly apprehend'st my wish.
At once would I depart—this very hour,
This very moment, if I am allow'd.
Time presses, *tempus fugit*, and the rest.      195
Couldst thou, sir, gaze within mine earnest heart,
Thou wouldst see reasons sound and selfless both—
Thou wouldst consider me a dear, close friend.

Mina      *[aside:]* I see how Seward plays a waiting game,
To let the madness come into the light.      200

Van Helsing      Canst thou not frankly tell thy reasons true?
Be wise and help us that we may help thee.

| | |
|---|---|
| Renfield | Professor, there is naught I may reply, |
| | For thou hast made an argument complete. |
| | Were I but free to speak, I would not pause,     205 |
| | Yet I am not the master of myself. |
| | 'Tis on thy trust alone I must rely. |

Seward      Let us depart. We have much work to do.

*[All but Renfield begin to leave.*

Renfield      Let me entreat thee, Doctor Seward, please!
Release me from this house of horrors now,     210
Send me away both how and where thou wilt,
Send keepers with me, arm'd with whips and chains,
Let them be escorts, let me legs be bound,
Take me to jail, but let me fly from here!
By all thou holdest sacred, let me go—     215
Save my poor spirit from eternal woe.
Wilt thou be senseless? Wilt thou never learn?
Seest not that I am sane and honest now,
No lunatic, yet fighting for my soul!
O hear me, hear me! Let me go anon!     220

Seward      No more of this. Get swiftly into bed,
Amend thy ill behavior, be discreet.

Renfield      Remember, Doctor Seward, that I tried
My hardest to convince thee of my words.

*[They leave the cell. Renfield remains, alone.*

Morris      Lest that man were endeavoring to bluff,     225
He is the sanest lunatic I've seen.

             'Twas clear his purpose was most serious—
             Couldst thou not one chance grant unto him, John?

Van Helsing    Except for that last outburst feverish,
             I would have set him free.

Arthur                —Yea, so would I.       230

Seward        'Tis possible that I agree with ye.
             Were that man's lunacy more ordinary,
             I would have ta'en a chance on trusting him.
             Yet he is so entangl'd with the Count
             That I fear e'en the tiniest misstep.      235
             I'll not forget how he begg'd for a cat,
             Then tried to tear my throat out with his teeth
             And call'd the Count his lord and master, too.
             'Tis possible he hopes to help the beast
             With some intention diabolical.        240
             If Dracula will call on rats and wolves,
             Shall he not summon madmen to his side?

Van Helsing    Sweet Mina, Jonathan: 'tis very late.
             You are too precious to forsake your rest.
             Your recent labors have been plentiful,    245
             And tiredness is showing on your faces—
             Thou, Jonathan, dost show a haggard face,
             And Mina, thou grow'st paler than the moon.
             Our work is ended for the nonce, methinks.
             You are our star and hope—pray, go upstairs   250
             And take the comfort of a night of rest.

Jonathan     Come, love, and to our room we shall retire
             That, in the morn, we may refreshèd be.

Mina           As you request, so shall it be. Farewell.

*[Exeunt Mina and Jonathan. Seward, Van Helsing,*
*Arthur and Morris confer.*

*Enter DRACULA, laughing, to RENFIELD's cell.*

Dracula  Dear friend, I come to visit thee again—  255
  Because thou welcom'dst me into this house,
  With joy may I return whene'er I will.

Renfield  My master, you have come! Not in the mist,
  Nor in the fog or shadows of the night,
  But solid, in the flesh! Why come you now?  260

Dracula  Behold my gift to thee, my loyal son.

*[Dracula waves his hand. A large moth flies into Renfield's cell.*
*Renfield seizes it.*

Renfield  The blood is life!

Dracula    —And more shalt thou enjoy:
  Rats in their hundred, thousands, millions too!
  Each one of them a life, with cats and dogs.
  Red blood, with which thou mayst have life fore'er— 265
  No more of buzzing flies. Thou, friend, shalt feast.
  Look past the window, to the field beyond.

Renfield  A mass of darkness o'er the grasses spread,
  That cometh on an 'twere a flame of fire.
  'Tis rats, abundant rats come for my meal!  270

Dracula  These lives I'll give thee, yea, through ev'ry age,
  If thou but worship me upon thy knees.

Renfield  My lord, my life, my master, my desire!
             *[Dracula moves closer to Renfield.*
    *[Aside:]* What is that scent that wafts about my cell.
    Is Missus Harker come to call again?    275

Dracula  Soon I shall come to thee again, my son.
    Until that time, be loyal, keen, and patient.

                *[Exit Dracula.*

Renfield  Pray, Doctor Seward, come! O, quickly come!
    *[Seward, Van Helsing, Arthur, and Morris reenter Renfield's cell.*
    O, I am dying—swiftly flees my life.
    The Count was here—just now!—he came to me  280
    And promis'd me the world for my allegiance.

Seward  Count Dracula, here? Arthur, Quincey, go!
    Search ye the grounds and see if he speaks true.

             *[Exit Arthur and Morris.*

Renfield  'Tis not, I fear, outside that ye should search.
    Where's Missus Harker? O, hear ye my words!  285
    When she was with ye some few moments hence,
    She was not as she was when first I saw her,
    But was like tea left too long in the pot—
    Dry, lacking life. Pale people I despise—
    I much prefer when folk are fill'd with blood,  290
    Yet she was like a desert, drain'd completely.

Van Helsing  What art thou saying?

Renfield      —He hath been at her!
    I smell'd her scent upon him even now,

Her fragrant blood enriching his foul veins.
He hath been drinking life from her, forsooth!  295

Seward      O, Abraham. Think'st thou this may be true?

Van Helsing  'Twas minutes since I call'd her pale of cheek.
If this be so, the monster hath prevail'd.

*Enter ARTHUR HOLMWOOD and QUINCEY MORRIS.*

Seward      By heaven, tell: what saw ye two outside?

Arthur      A fog so thick that little could be seen,  300
Yet I did seem to spy rats scampering.

Morris      Their little legs escaping rapidly—
'Twas more like seeing visions in a dream.

Van Helsing  The Count?

Arthur              —I saw him not.

Morris                  —Nay, nor did I.

Seward      What of the Harkers? Are they gone to bed?  305

Arthur      Indeed, and likely lock'd their chamber door.

Morris      What of it? If the Count already fled,
'Tis well the Harkers safely are within.

Van Helsing  Poor Mina may the Count's next victim be.

Arthur      Good God!

| | | |
|---|---|---|
| Morris | —Shall grief surround us evermore? | 310 |

Seward      We must unto their chamber presently.

Van Helsing      In troth, we know the worst now, gentlemen:
He's here, we know his purpose and his aim.
This patient hath the monster welcom'd in,
And Madam Harker is his newfound target.      315
Let us take arms, for danger be prepar'd—
Yet lose no time; no instant may be spar'd.

*[Exeunt.*

## SCENE 3.

*London. The Harkers' room in the asylum. Night.*

*Enter MINA HARKER and JONATHAN HARKER, in their bedchamber.*

Mina      How pleasant 'tis to rest the weary head,
Which is confounded with a thousand trials.

Jonathan      No other partner in the marriage bed
Would I desire, not for one million miles.

Mina      Good night, my love, and may thy dreams be sweet,      5
With naught to trouble or disrupt thy slumber.

Jonathan      Until the morn, when we the sun shall greet:
Rest well, and let no worries thee encumber.

*[They rest. Jonathan shuts his eyes, Mina lies awake.*

Mina      Though I took Doctor Seward's sleeping draught,
My mind is wakeful, restless, and afeard.      10
A myriad of fancies horrible

Begin to crowd upon my busy mind,
Of blood and pain, of vampires, trouble, death.
Be resolute now, Mina—find the sleep
That hath alluded thee these many nights.                 15


*She tries to sleep. Enter DRACULA, unseen, wrapped in mist.*


Dracula        *[aside:]* Let that poor fool, her husband, slumber on—
               My power over him is absolute,
               And he shall never know that I am here.


Mina           Behold, the same white mist that, many nights,
               Hath been a constant presence in this room.          20
               The terror that the simple mist conveys
               Is like a chill of winter in late spring.
               O Jonathan, art thou awake, my love?
                                       *[Mina tries to stir Jonathan.*
               He sleepeth like a hibernating bear,
               Who shall not rouse or wake for many months.         25
               'Tis like 'twas he who took the sleeping draught,
               And I had ta'en a brew for wakefulness.
               The window, which is resting open now—
               Was it not closèd when we came abed?


                                       *[Dracula steps out of the mist.*


Dracula        My lady, thou art mine and I am thine.                30


Mina           *[aside:]* The tall, thin man, with lips of richest red,
               The nose of hawk, the waxen face most pale,
               The sharp white teeth—'tis just as they describ'd!
               'Tis Dracula who stands afore me here!


Dracula        Be silent! If thou mak'st the smallest sound,         35
               I'll dash his brains before thy very eyes.

Exertion plenty hath been mine of late—
Refreshment I deserve, to quench my thirst.
'Tis not the first or second time that I
Have taken nourishment from thy pure veins.            40

Mina            *[aside:]* O, wherefore doth my spirit not protest?
I would not stop him—'tis his victims' curse!
                        *[Dracula stoops and drinks from her neck.*
What woe, what bliss, his lips upon my throat!
My strength is fading like the setting sun.

Dracula            Thou, like so many others, would attempt            45
To match wits with a pow'rful, ancient mind.
Thou help'st these feeble men to prey on me,
And frustrate my mysterious designs.
Soon shall ye know what 'tis to cross my path.
Their energies they waste, to pick at me            50
Like sparrows pecking at a mustard seed—
I who have conquer'd and commanded nations.
Now thou, my dear, art flesh of mine own flesh,
Now thou, my love, art blood of mine own blood,
Kin of my kin, companion, helpmeet too,            55
My winepress bountiful whereon I drink.
In time, thou shalt be queen where I am king,
And all shall fall upon their knees for thee
And minister unto thine ev'ry need.
First, thou must punish'd be for waywardness,            60
For aiding them in hindering my schemes.
When my brain speaketh "Come!" unto thy mind,
Thou shalt cross land or sea to do my will.
To make it so, to make thee mine fore'er,
Thou must take nourishment e'en as I do.            65
            *[Dracula bears his chest and scratches himself, then pulls Mina toward his*
                        *blood. She drinks.*

Drink of the sustenance I give to thee,
Drink of the blood in which thou art baptiz'd,
Drink of the tincture of eternity,
Drink of the life that lasts forevermore!

*Enter ABRAHAM VAN HELSING, JOHN SEWARD,*
*ARTHUR HOLMWOOD, and QUINCEY MORRIS,*
*breaking through the chamber door.*

Van Helsing    The Count! 'Tis he, for it can be none else!    70

Morris    What is he doing, clutching at her so?

Dracula    Abhorrent men, who interrupt the feast!
Taste thou the cold dish of my sweet revenge!
*[Dracula leaps at them. Van Helsing holds up a consecrated wafer.*
Alas, the power of the sacred host—
It burneth on my skin an 'twere aflame.    75
Ye triumph for the moment, but be sure:
Count Dracula shall have his vengeance yet!

*[Exit Dracula in mist, throwing Mina onto the bed.*

Arthur    He vanisheth, like water turn'd to steam
That dissipates and fadeth in a trice!

Morris    Perchance I may pursue the brigand hence!    80

*[Exit Morris in pursuit.*

Mina    Alack, my life! My woe! What have I done?

Seward    Behold the blood that trickles down her neck.
For certain, Dracula hath drunk from her.

| | | |
|---|---|---|
| Van Helsing | Friend Jonathan is in a stupor, such | |
| | As our foul foe, the vampire, can produce. | 85 |
| | We must wake him whilst Madam Mina doth | |
| | Recover her own senses. Jonathan! | |

*[Van Helsing takes water from the bedside and drips it on Jonathan's face.*

| | | |
|---|---|---|
| Jonathan | What is it? Have I too long been a-slumber? | |
| Mina | Dear God, what horrors have I seen tonight? | |
| Jonathan | What is the matter, Mina? Why this blood? | 90 |
| | By heaven, hath it come, at last, to this? | |
| | Friends, help her if ye can! What happen'd here? | |
| Van Helsing | Be still and, pray, attend unto thy wife. | |
| | My lady, we are here; no enemy | |
| | Shall visit thee whilst we are by thy side. | 95 |
| | We must be calm and counsel take together. | |
| Mina | Unclean, unclean! I swallow'd from his breast— | |
| | Count Dracula's blood hath infected me. | |
| | My Jonathan, we two must kiss no more— | |
| | 'Tis I who, now, thou hast most cause to fear. | 100 |
| Jonathan | Nay, Mina, I shall not thy words obey. | |
| | May I be judg'd and suffer more than e'er | |
| | If anything betwixt us ever come. | |
| | Please, Doctor Seward, tell me what occurr'd. | |
| Seward | The patient, Renfield, had encounter with | 105 |
| | The Count, upon whose self was Mina's scent. | |
| | This Renfield call'd us back once ye did leave | |
| | And warn'd us that the Count had drunk of her. | |
| | We came as quickly as our feet could run | |

<table>
<tr><td></td><td>And found thy Mina drinking from the Count,</td><td>110</td></tr>
<tr><td></td><td>As he had supp'd from her, which thou canst see</td><td></td></tr>
<tr><td></td><td>By those two pinpricks on the lady's neck.</td><td></td></tr>
<tr><td>Mina</td><td>O, Jonathan, forgive me!</td><td></td></tr>
<tr><td>Jonathan</td><td>     —Mina, love—</td><td></td></tr>
<tr><td></td><td>No wrong has thou committed knowingly.</td><td></td></tr>
</table>

*Enter QUINCEY MORRIS.*

<table>
<tr><td>Morris</td><td>I could not find the villain anywhere.</td><td>115</td></tr>
<tr><td></td><td>The passage or the study, all the rooms—</td><td></td></tr>
<tr><td></td><td>Though he had been within, now is he fled.</td><td></td></tr>
<tr><td></td><td>I saw a bat flap westward through the night,</td><td></td></tr>
<tr><td></td><td>Not unto Carfax, but—if 'twere the Count—</td><td></td></tr>
<tr><td></td><td>Toward some other, undiscover'd lair.</td><td>120</td></tr>
<tr><td></td><td>The morning sky doth redden in the east,</td><td></td></tr>
<tr><td></td><td>The dawn is near; thus, he shall not return.</td><td></td></tr>
<tr><td>Arthur</td><td>What is his plan? What thinkest thou, professor?</td><td></td></tr>
<tr><td>Van Helsing</td><td>He is experimenting, taking time—</td><td></td></tr>
<tr><td></td><td>A man who liveth many centuries</td><td>125</td></tr>
<tr><td></td><td>Can well afford to wait and slowly move:</td><td></td></tr>
<tr><td></td><td>*Festina lente* may well be his motto.</td><td></td></tr>
<tr><td></td><td>First did he use the patient, Renfield, as</td><td></td></tr>
<tr><td></td><td>His entry point and most devoted pupil.</td><td></td></tr>
<tr><td></td><td>Now he to Madam Mina turns his sights,</td><td>130</td></tr>
<tr><td></td><td>Yet knoweth that he must by night progress.</td><td></td></tr>
<tr><td></td><td>His strategy withal the many caskets</td><td></td></tr>
<tr><td></td><td>Is to allow himself the freedom of</td><td></td></tr>
<tr><td></td><td>Full many places where he can reside,</td><td></td></tr>
<tr><td></td><td>Belike throughout the whole extent of London.</td><td>135</td></tr>
<tr><td></td><td>Yea, he is learning, plotting ev'ry move.</td><td></td></tr>
</table>

| | | |
|---|---|---|
| Mina | There must be no concealment twixt we six; | |
| | Already hath there been too much suppress'd. | |
| | Think me no shrinking violet that ye | |
| | Must cover from the harsh light of the sun— | 140 |
| | I shall be ready for whatever comes. | |
| | | |
| Van Helsing | But Madam Mina, art thou not afeard— | |
| | Not only for thyself, but for the others, | |
| | Considering the terrors thou hast fac'd? | |
| | | |
| Mina | Nay, for my mind is finally decided. | 145 |
| | | |
| Arthur | What meanest thou? | |
| | | |
| Mina | —Should I find any sign | |
| | Within myself of some intent to harm | |
| | Those whom I love, I swear that I shall die. | |
| | | |
| Jonathan | Thou canst not mean that thou wouldst slay thyself? | |
| | | |
| Mina | Most gladly would I, if I had no friend | 150 |
| | Who lov'd me plentif'lly enow to save | |
| | Me such a pain and do the deed himself. | |
| | | |
| Jonathan | Would that I could destroy his earthy life, | |
| | And send the Count to hell eternally! | |
| | | |
| Mina | Nay, say not so, my dearest Jonathan: | 155 |
| | It may yet be that I shall someday need | |
| | The selfsame pity thou wouldst show him not— | |
| | To slay with mercy, that my soul may fly | |
| | Unto the waiting arms of heav'n above, | |
| | And not to kill with vengeance, heartlessly, | 160 |
| | And sentence me to everlasting torment. | |

Should it be so, I hope that I shall find
So brave a friend, as Lucy did in Arthur.

Van Helsing   Cease we this talk of death and anguish, Mina:
Thou must not die by thine or any hand.                    165
Until the other—who hath stain'd thy life—
Is truly dead, thou must remain alive,
Lest thou should, like the demon, be undead.
Yea, thou must live! Endeavor to survive,
Though death may seem a boon unspeakable.                  170
Upon thy soul, I charge thee: do not die,
Nor think of death, until this evil's pass'd!

Mina   I promise, friend, if God doth let me live,
Long shall I strive to do so faithfully.
Perchance, when comes that final, fateful day,            175
This present horror may have pass'd away.

*[Exeunt.*

*Enter DRACULA on balcony.*

Dracula   You think to baffle me, ye mortal wisps,
With faces pale like sheep in butchers' shops,
Lin'd up for slaughter, weak and laughable.
You shall be sorry yet, each one of you!                  180
Search to destroy me, yet I shall arise—
My work is done in centuries, not days.
O, how I shall enjoy the flavor of
This horrid plot, this earth, this pit, this England.
Throughout the globe entire I'll freely roam             185
And feast your women, slay your men at home!

*[Exit.*

# SCENE 4.

*London. An asylum. Day.*

*Enter MINA HARKER as Chorus.*

| | |
|---|---|
| Mina | The sun that rose upon our sorrow gave |
| | Its light and clarity unto our aim: |
| | For those few daylight hours the Count was wholly |
| | Confinèd to his earthly envelope— |
| | We had all day to hunt and purify |

The sun that rose upon our sorrow gave
Its light and clarity unto our aim:
For those few daylight hours the Count was wholly
Confinèd to his earthly envelope—
We had all day to hunt and purify
The caskets that he made his wickèd lairs.
That day went by, and others like it, too,
And we destroy'd the caskets one by one.
Van Helsing, to protect my soul from spoil,
Did touch my forehead with the sacred host—
The consecrated wafer of our faith—
Which doing so, did burn into my flesh
As if it were a piece of white-hot metal.
No sign show'd I of sharper, growing teeth—
But time was short, and there was time for fear.
The host was also us'd when we found caskets:
Together, we would open wide the lid,
Preparing to meet Dracula therein,
Yet, finding each one still unoccupied,
Van Helsing plac'd a wafer on the dirt
To purify the soil that lay within—
Then would we nail the casket clos'd fore'er
And know we'd taken one more home from him.
One after th'other did we do our work,
That first morn turning into days and weeks.
In total, caskets forty-nine we cleans'd,
Yet one eludes us still, wheree'er we look.
Van Helsing, thus, shall come to me today
And hypnotize my mind—link'd to the Count's—
That we may see where he hath hid himself.

Such is the final hope of our attack,
Such is the means by which we'll hunt the beast.

*Enter JONATHAN HARKER, ABRAHAM VAN HELSING,*
*JOHN SEWARD, ARTHUR HOLMWOOD, and QUINCEY MORRIS.*

| | |
|---|---|
| Van Helsing | Let us proceed at once, my worthy friends—<br>Bear witness to the op'ning of her mind. |
| Jonathan | Art thou most certain, love, of this new scheme?    35 |
| Mina | We have no other hope; let us begin. |
| Van Helsing | Watch thou my finger, wheresoe'er it moves—<br>Thine eyes grow tir'd, thy thoughts are pliable,<br>Thy mind shall open unto my requests,<br>Thy spirit shall embrace my presence there.    40 |
| Arthur | *[aside:]* Her eyes are clos'd, she sits as still as ice—<br>'Tis only by her gentle breathing that<br>I know she is alive. |
| Van Helsing |       —Now ope thine eyne,<br>And be the vessel wherein truth is held. |
| Morris | *[aside:]* Her eyes are open, yet she is not there:    45<br>She seemeth wholly like another woman,<br>Her vacant gaze is empty, faraway. |
| Van Helsing | Where art thou? |
| Mina |       —Verily, I do not know:<br>Sleep hath no place that it can call its own. |

*[Van Helsing motions to Seward.*

Seward        *[aside:]* He bids me part the curtain to reveal        50
              A hint of sunlight from the day without.

                            *[Seward opens the curtain to let in some light.*

Van Helsing   Where art thou now?

Mina                        —'Tis strange; I cannot tell.

Van Helsing   What canst thou see?

Mina                        —But darkness all around.

Van Helsing   What dost thou hear?

Mina                        —The lapping of the waves,
              Which gurgle past in little leaping sprays.        55

Van Helsing   Art thou aboard a ship?

Mina                        —In faith, I am!

Van Helsing   What else canst hear?

Mina                        —The sound of folk o'erhead,
              Whose feet are stamping as they run about.
              The creaking of a chain, which clangeth as
              The capstan falls into the ratchet's hold.        60

Van Helsing   What art thou doing?

Mina                        —Lying still as death.

Jonathan   *[aside:]* Poor Mina, I'd not have her dwell within
      This madman's mind. *[Aloud:]* Professor, be thou swift!

        *[Van Helsing puts his hands on Mina's shoulders.*

Van Helsing  Awake, my brave, dear woman. Come thou back.

Mina     *[waking:]* Have I been talking to ye in my sleep?  65

Van Helsing  No moment may we lose—'tis not too late.
      That ship was weighing anchor whilst she spoke,
      Departing from the Port of London now.
      The Count doth know he hath one earth-box left,
      And that we trail as hounds do chase the fox.  70
      He takes his final casket on a ship,
      And leaves the land, imagining escape.
      But nay, we stalk him onward. Tally ho!

Mina     Why seek him further if he doth depart?

Van Helsing  Now more than ever must we find the rogue,  75
      E'en if we follow to the jaws of hell!

Jonathan   Yet why, professor?

Van Helsing     —He may live fore'er,
      But Mina is a mortal woman still.
      Time now is to be dreaded, ever since
      He put his hateful mark upon her throat.  80
      The pow'r of the undead is passing strange—
      The forces of th'occult do operate
      Upon the physical in ways peculiar.
      He hath infected Mina—pray, forgive
      That I speak truths so bluntly; know that I  85
      Am thinking only of thy lasting good.

If he no more doth feast on Mina's blood,
She only needs to live as e'er she hath—
The seed is planted in her very soul.
For, when death comes, she shall be made like him.     90
This must not be—thus we must follow on:
In Transylvania waits our final scene!

Morris          Perish the one whose mind is backward now!

Van Helsing     Thou dost not wish more help from England, Quincey? 95

Morris          God's will! My friend, would thou and I alone,
Without more help, could fight this noble battle!

Mina          Come, let us make our preparations swift.

*[Exeunt, manet Van Helsing.*

Van Helsing     The truth I would not speak within their presence
Is that I spy new signs on Mina's face:               100
The features of the vampire grow in her.
'Tis now but slight, yet those who know may see:
Her canine teeth grow sharper by degree,
Her eyes are harder, losing energy.
E'en more, though, is the danger to her soul—         105
She is more quiet than she was before,
Like Lucy ere the woman perishèd.
If we may, through her mind, behold the Count,
May not the Count see us by selfsame means?
To Castle Dracula we make all speed,                  110
That from his grasp brave Mina may be freed.

*[Exit.*

# SCENE 5.

*Transylvania and Castle Dracula.*

*Enter MINA HARKER and JONATHAN HARKER.*

Mina — Dear Jonathan, as we make this campaign
Against the dreaded Count, our horrid foe,
Methought at first my presence was a bane—
For what if he doth know all I do know?

Jonathan — Sweet Mina, if 'tis that which worries thee,    5
Thy presence, at the last, we should omit.

Mina — Like ship that moves by rudder on the sea,
My mind hath chang'd its course: it is more fit
For me to travel with ye to the end.
'Tis only thus our band of friends is safe.    10

Jonathan — Straight into danger's way must we descend,
Against the Count's aggression shall we chafe.

Mina — Yet trust that I have reasons of mine own.

Jonathan — I hear thee; we shall not leave thee alone.

*Enter ABRAHAM VAN HELSING, JOHN SEWARD,*
*ARTHUR HOLMWOOD, and QUINCEY MORRIS.*

Van Helsing — Are all prepar'd? Today shall be the day,    15
To bind us, or undo us, one of them.

Morris — Should I the vile box see, I shall not wait—
I shall destroy the monster suddenly,
E'en though a thousand foes could see me do't
And, by the doing, I would seal my doom.    20

Van Helsing   Spake like a good and brave combatant, Quincey.

Mina   We hither have arriv'd in freedom, friends,
Perchance 'twill be our final time together.
I know ye shall be with me to the end,
Yet bear in mind I am not as ye are:                    25
There is a poison in my blood, my soul,
Which may defeat me sans a remedy.
One further thing I humbly beg of ye.

Arthur   What is it, Mina?

Mina                    —If I should be slain,
Set free my spirit, as ye did for Lucy.                 30
Or, if the time requires, before my death,
Consent to kill me.

Seward                 —When may that time come?

Mina   When you shall be convinc'd I am so chang'd
That 'tis far better I should die than live.
Drive, then, the stake through my still-beating heart,  35
Cut off my head sans mercy or delay.
Whatever is demanded, give me rest.

Jonathan   And must I promise this, my darling wife?

Mina   Thou too, my dearest—be thou bold, shrink not.

*[They swear.*

Van Helsing   Smart lass, and better than the best of us.     40
As we proceed, let us review our state:
Count Dracula is fled toward his home,

Realizing that he hath one casket left.
Evasive hath he been—although we have
Determin'd he doth travel t'ward the east,    45
He may yet travel by full many means.
Our task must be to find him on the way,
Stop him from reaching Castle Dracula,
To keep him from his worser pow'rs at home.

Mina           I have deduc'd the ways he may be ta'en:    50
By road, directly through the Borgo Pass,
By water on the Pruth or Sereth rivers.
'Tis best if we split forces in pursuit,
That we may find him ere he reach the castle.

Morris        Come, John, and let us venture by the Pruth,    55
Perchance to catch him by the northmost route.

Seward        Long hath we hunted deer together, Morris—
Today we stalk far larger, fiercer game.

[Exeunt Seward and Morris.

Van Helsing   Friend Jonathan, although thou wouldst not part
From thy belovèd Mina, go with Arthur:    60
Take ye the southern route, along the Sereth—
Ye are both young men, stronger for the task.
I shall with Mina through the Borgo Pass,
Direct toward the center of his might.

Jonathan     Although the separation works me woe,    65
Thy reason is apparent; I shall go.

Mina           Farewell, dear husband, till again meet we—
My latest, truest thoughts are e'er for thee.

*[Exeunt Jonathan and Arthur. Mina and Van Helsing begin to walk.*

| | | |
|---|---|---|
| Van Helsing | I fain would hypnotize thee once again, | |
| | To learn whate'er we can of Dracula. | 70 |

Mina      Thrice have we this procedure underta'en,
Which led us here—I'll not refuse a fourth.

Van Helsing      Watch thou my finger, wheresoe'er it moves—
Thine eyes grow tir'd, thy thoughts are pliable,
Thy mind shall open unto my requests,      75
Thy spirit welcome in my presence there.

> *[Mina does not fall into a trance.*

Alas, the spell hath not had its effect.
The power fadeth with each passing day—
As we approach, my potency grows dim.

Mina      Fear not, professor—lo, this is the way.      80

Van Helsing      How dost thou know it?

Mina      —Is't not evident?
By this route Jonathan first travel'd here.
His writings I have read so often that
I feel as I have seen the path myself.

Van Helsing      Let us proceed, then, cleverest of women.      85

> *[Exeunt Mina and Van Helsing.*

*Enter JOHN SEWARD and QUINCEY MORRIS, rowing the Pruth.*

Seward      The river takes us southward speedily;
Methinks we'll reach the castle by the morrow.

Morris        Let us employ the strength of our two backs,
              The sooner to catch up the villain there!

                                              *[Exeunt.*

         *Enter JONATHAN HARKER and ARTHUR HOLMWOOD*
                        *on the Sereth.*

Arthur        The sun completes its journey to the west—        90
              Pray God for safety after it hath set.

Jonathan      O, how my heart doth tremble in my breast
              To venture t'ward the castle where I was
              Held prisoner, sans hope, lock'd tight with fear.

Arthur        Take courage, Jonathan, your friends go with thee:     95
              Thou art not now, nor ne'er shall be, alone.

                                              *[Exeunt.*

         *Enter MINA HARKER and ABRAHAM VAN HELSING.*

Van Helsing   We'll stop to rest awhile ere we march forth;
              We both are growing weary with each step.
              The night comes on, and we must pause to sleep.

Mina          The castle riseth in the distance now—        100
              It cannot be a mile till we are there.

              *[Van Helsing draws a circle in the snow around Mina.*

Van Helsing   This circle I inscribe shall safety grant—
              Around the ring the sacred host I wave,
              That heaven may protect us as we rest.

| | | |
|---|---|---|
| Mina | I feel as weak as I have ever felt. | 105 |

| | |
|---|---|
| Van Helsing | *[aside:]* How wan she looks; his pow'r o'er her is strong. |

*Enter THREE WOMEN.*

| | |
|---|---|
| Mina | Seest thou these creatures, beautiful of form? |

| | |
|---|---|
| Van Helsing | Stay thou within the ring—go not without, |
| | For here, within, thy safety is assur'd. |

| | | |
|---|---|---|
| Mina | My safety? Ha! 'Tis thou for whom I fear— | 110 |
| | None safer in the world from them than I. | |

| | |
|---|---|
| Woman 2 | Come, my lovely, with us join, |
| | We have juices to purloin. |

| | | |
|---|---|---|
| Woman 1 | I smell thine enticing scent— | |
| | Full blood-sister, make assent. | 115 |

| | |
|---|---|
| Woman 3 | Pleasures shalt thou know anon, |
| | Carnal pleasures for his spawn! |

| | |
|---|---|
| Woman 1 | Master nearly hath arriv'd, |
| | Soon his pow'r shall be reviv'd. |

| | | |
|---|---|---|
| Woman 3 | Whilst he's gone, we'll sup on men— | 120 |
| | Till he cometh back again. | |

| | |
|---|---|
| Woman 2 | Come, my sister, comrade, pet, |
| | Much of joy waits for thee yet! |

| | | |
|---|---|---|
| Van Helsing | Away, ye demons sent from hell below— | |
| | And trouble not our slumber. See the ring! | 125 |

By sacred rites we make our sure defense—
Go, evil bastions, hence unto thy realm.

*[Exeunt women.*

Mina       How shall we sleep, with evil hereabout?

Van Helsing       The circle shall protect us, by my troth.

*[Exeunt.*

*Enter JONATHAN HARKER and ARTHUR HOLMWOOD, debarking.*

Jonathan       Now dawns the final morning of our quest.       130

Arthur       The castle on the cliff—I see it now!

Jonathan       My love, mine enemy, my allies all—
Draws nigh the hour when it is finishèd.

*[Exeunt.*

*Enter JOHN SEWARD and QUINCEY MORRIS on horseback.*

Morris       The Pruth behind us, now with speed we ride.
The daylight calls us onward to the fight!       135

Seward       Would that we were already in the fray!
The castle waiteth on the far horizon.

*[Exeunt.*

*Enter MINA HARKER, sleeping. Enter ABRAHAM VAN HELSING in
the castle graveyard nearby.*

| | |
|---|---|
| Van Helsing | The sun doth grant the hours when we may work. |
| | Brave Mina lies within the circle still— |
| | Asleep and weak, her soul in safety resting—    140 |
| | Whilst I approach the graveyard where I must |
| | Discover where the beastly women lie. |
| | Nay, nay, I should not call them "women," for |
| | True women are full worthy of respect: |
| | They are the books, the arts, the academes,    145 |
| | That show, contain and nourish all the world. |
| | These monsters shall not by their name be call'd. |
| | A-ha! Here are the caskets where they lie. |
| | Be swift, be blunt, as hammer is to nail! |

*[Van Helsing opens the caskets one by one and drives a stake through the heart
of each of the Dracula's minions.*

    One—for dear Mina, who is languishing!    150
    Two—for sweet Lucy, prematurely ta'en!
    Three—for the victims through the centuries!
    'Tis butcher's work! See how they scream and flail,
    Yet quickly as the stake doth pierce their heart
    Each one doth crumble, vanishing to dust.    155
    The death they should have died in time agone
    Arriveth and declareth, "I am here!"

| | |
|---|---|
| Mina | *[waking:]* Professor, come thou from that fearful place. |
| | My husband doth approach, I feel him near! |

| | |
|---|---|
| Van Helsing | *[aside:]* Alas, I know not who it is she means—    160 |
| | The look of wildness in her sunken eyes |
| | Suggests she means the Count, not Jonathan. |

*Enter a carriage driven by two SZGANY SERVANTS, rushing toward the
castle and bearing a casket in which DRACULA lies.*

    *[Aloud:]* Look, Madam Mina, now the Count doth come,
    Borne by a carriage from the mouth of hell!

| | | |
|---|---|---|
| Mina | How hath another day already fled? | 165 |
| | The evening draweth on; the end comes nigh. | |
| | At sunset shall the thing—imprison'd now | |
| | Within the casket that the coach doth bear— | |
| | Break forth, take awful form, and flee or, worse, | |
| | Destroy us as we seek to conquer it. | 170 |
| | | |
| Van Helsing | See how they flog the horses, galloping | |
| | As swiftly as they may toward the castle. | |
| | They race for dusk. Alas, are we too late? | |

*Enter JOHN SEWARD and QUINCEY MORRIS on horses,*
*pursuing the carriage.*

| | | |
|---|---|---|
| Mina | Behold, two horsemen follow on apace! | |
| | | |
| Van Helsing | They have the forms of John and Quincey—ha! | 175 |
| | Let us descend at once, to catch them up. | |

*Enter JONATHAN HARKER and ARTHUR HOLMWOOD,*
*also pursuing the carriage.*

| | | |
|---|---|---|
| Mina | Two more, which brings the number now to four— | |
| | How like the horsemen of th'apocalypse | |
| | They seem to me, which bring both weal and woe. | |
| | | |
| Van Helsing | 'Tis Jonathan and Arthur— | |
| | | |
| Mina | —O, my love! | 180 |
| | | |
| Van Helsing | To them, at once! They shall converge anon | |
| | E'en at the castle gates—the time hath come! | |

*[Mina and Van Helsing run toward the castle. Jonathan, Morris, Seward,*
*and Arthur block the carriage's path.*

| | |
|---|---|
| Jonathan | *[to the Szgany:]* Halt, minsters of death! |

| | |
|---|---|
| Morris | —Cease your dread flight! |

*[One of the Szgany leaps from the carriage and fights with Morris,*
*cutting him with the knife. Morris subdues him.*

| | |
|---|---|
| Arthur | *[arriving:]* Our poniards and our muskets ready stand. |

Seward      One movement further and we shall attack.      185

*[The Szgany freeze.*

Szgany 1      *[aside:]* Alas, that we poor servants of this Count—
Who holds us not by will, but poverty—
Should come to be oppress'd by English men!

Jonathan      Come, Quincey—to the casket speedily.

Morris      Indeed. Let us not lose the name of action.      190

Arthur      We'll guard the servants whilst ye do the deed.

*[Jonathan and Morris lower the casket from the carriage to the ground.*
*Jonathan opens the casket with his knife.*

Seward      Count Dracula is like a waxen image,
His eyes with hatred fill'd e'en as he sleeps.

Mina      *[arriving:]* O, Jonathan! Be swift, my love, be swift.
The sun below the mountaintops doth fall.      195

Van Helsing    *[arriving:]* The shadows fall upon us presently.
               There is no time to lose—strike, gentlemen!

Jonathan       The moment for my sure revenge hath come—
               When I repay the fiend for what he's done.

Morris         Be strong and sudden, Jonathan. For Lucy!          200

*[Dracula's eyes widen as he wakes. Jonathan cuts his throat and Morris drives
a stake through his heart.*

Jonathan       The final stroke, for precious Mina's sake!

Morris         The final nail, for all who have been slain!

Dracula        *[dying:]* If one good deed in all my life I did,
               I do repent it from my very soul.

*[Dracula dies.*

Mina           See—peace profound doth wash o'er his dread face,  205
               As centuries of sin depart his soul.

Van Helsing    His body crumbles as his minions' did.
               'Tis well. Our labors here are ended, friends.

*[Exeunt the Szgany servants, fleeing. Morris falls.*

Seward         Brave Quincey—what befalls thee? Art thou hurt?

Arthur         The rogue attack'd him when the coach arriv'd;     210
               Methought I saw a blade catch Quincey's side.

Mina           Speak, Quincey. Thou art here, among thy friends.

Morris      I only am too happy to have been  
Of any service—death was worth this moment.  
See, Mina, how the blush comes to thy cheek:    215  
Thank heaven that our work is not in vain—  
The snow is not more stainless than thy soul,  
And where the host did sear thy forehead once  
The wound is heal'd—the curse hath pass'd away!  
The promise of the new Jerusalem    220  
Hath been fulfill'd on Transylvania's shores.  
In this Jerusalem shall Quincey die.

*[Morris dies.*

Van Helsing      A gallant, noble man before us lies,  
Whose soul doth now unto the fates arise.

*[All freeze. Mina addresses the audience as Epilogue.*

Mina      'Twas seven years ago we pass'd through flame,    225  
The forge's fire refining friendship's name.  
The happiness of some of us, now cur'd,  
Is worth the pain that our bold band endur'd.  
A son was born to us, our joy and pride,  
Upon the day that Quincey Morris died.    230  
Methinks his courage—none had greater since he—  
Hath pass'd into our boy, whom we nam'd Quincey.  
In time, to Translyvania we return'd,  
Tread ground that, in our memories, was burn'd.  
Each trace of our adventure was remov'd,    235  
The castle desolate, our feats unprov'd.  
Van Helsing says, "We need no evidence;  
We ask none to believe our tale intense.  
This boy will, someday, know his mother's strength,  
Her bravery and wisdom, tried at length."    240  
His words are kindness, serving as a balm,

A garnish to our life of quiet calm.
For my part, I desire my child may know
None of the troubles that brought us such woe.
When he is old enow, we'll tell, in whole,       245
The story of the men who sav'd my soul.
Then shall he understand what was at stake:
They lov'd me, and they dar'd much for my sake.

*[Exeunt omnes.*

# AFTERWORD

Dracula, as a character, is inescapable in modern western culture. My first encounter with the Count was probably the campy 1979 movie *Love at First Bite*, which my parents owned on VHS. Francis Ford Coppola's *Bram Stoker's Dracula*—the film a friend recently described as "one of the truest and yet one of the most bizarre adaptations ever"—came along in 1992. I saw it in the theater that fall with the other 15-year-olds. But I didn't read the novel until last year, when the *Dracula Daily* email list delivered the journal entries, letters, and newspaper clippings through which Bram Stoker told his story to my inbox from May through November.

Those who know Bram Stoker's novel well will recognize that—by necessity—the book has been cut and simplified. This is especially true in the fifth act, where the hunt for Dracula's caskets and the journey to Castle Dracula is greatly condensed. A novella like *Strange Case of Dr. Jekyll and Mr. Hyde* is so short that it allows for a comprehensive adaptation, but *Dracula*—about six times as long as *Jekyll and Hyde*—requires intense narrative decision-making. For you *Dracula* stalwarts out there, I hope the cuts make sense.

My biggest surprise, after writing this adaptation, is how little we see of Dracula himself. He doesn't have any spoken lines between Act I and Act V (though he appears onstage with no dialogue in two scenes). His death happens quickly and—in the book—he says nothing when he dies. The six protagonists who hunt him and his servant Renfield are all larger parts.

Any time I write a Shakespearean adaptation—this is my twenty-third!—I decide what name to use for characters' cue lines (their name as it appears before they speak). This was difficult for *Dracula*, because some characters are more known by their last names—Seward and Van Helsing especially—while others are known by their first, like Mina, Jonathan, and Arthur. I decided to use the names that Bram Stoker most often uses for each character, which means the cue lines have a mix of first and last names. It's inconsistent, I know, but I couldn't imagine referring to Van Helsing as "Abraham" throughout or referring to Mina as "Murray" or "M. Harker." Those of you who desire consistency, forgive me.

Speaking of names: I chose to maintain Bram Stoker's spelling of places and geographical features (e.g., Buda-pesth and the Sereth river) rather than change them to reflect modern spellings. The asylum where John Seward works is never named in the book, so it's not named in the play.

This is the third and final play in my Shakespearean horror trilogy, after *Frankenstein* and *Jekyll and Hyde*. It's also the one I feared most, its sweeping tale far longer than the other two (*Dracula* is nearly double the length of *Frankenstein*). It is, therefore, also the longest of the three plays. Now the trilogy is complete, and—with any luck—Shakespeare is a little scarier.

—September 12, 2022
Portland, Oregon

**Ian Doescher** is the *New York Times* bestselling author of the *William Shakespeare Star Wars* series, the Pop Shakespeare series, the children's poetry collection *I Wish I Had a Wookiee*, and other books. He lives in Portland, Oregon with his spouse Jennifer, teenagers Liam and Graham, and dog Thorfinn. Find Ian online at iandoescher.com.